D0450964

Scout's Honor

Book
4

Stan Rogow Productions • Grosset & Dunlap

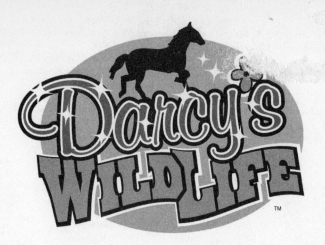

Scout's Honor

Book 4

By Jory Simms

Based on the television series
created by Doug Tuber and Tim Maile

Stan Rogow Productions • Grosset & Dunlap

GROSSET & DUNLAP
Published by the Penguin Group
Penguin Group (USA) Inc., 375 Hudson Street, New York, New York 10014, U.S.A.
Penguin Group (Canada), 90 Eglinton Avenue East, Suite 700, Toronto, Ontario,
Canada M4P 2Y3 (a division of Pearson Penguin Canada Inc.)
Penguin Books Ltd, 80 Strand, London WC2R 0RL, England
Penguin Ireland, 25 St Stephen's Green, Dublin 2, Ireland
(a division of Penguin Books Ltd)
Penguin Group (Australia), 250 Camberwell Road, Camberwell, Victoria 3124, Australia
(a division of Pearson Australia Group Pty Ltd)
Penguin Books India Pvt Ltd, 11 Community Centre, Panchsheel Park,
New Delhi - 110 017, India
Penguin Group (NZ), Cnr Airborne and Rosedale Roads, Albany, Auckland 1310,
New Zealand (a division of Pearson New Zealand Ltd)
Penguin Books (South Africa) (Pty) Ltd, 24 Sturdee Avenue, Rosebank, Johannesburg
2196, South Africa

Penguin Books Ltd, Registered Offices:
80 Strand, London WC2R 0RL, England

If you purchased this book without a cover, you should be aware that this book is stolen
property. It was reported as "unsold and destroyed" to the publisher, and neither the
author nor the publisher has received any payment for this "stripped book."

The scanning, uploading, and distribution of this book via the Internet or via any
other means without the permission of the publisher is illegal and punishable by law.
Please purchase only authorized electronic editions, and do not participate in or
encourage electronic piracy of copyrighted materials.
Your support of the author's rights is appreciated.

The publisher does not have any control over and does not assume any responsibility
for author or third-party websites or their content.

Text copyright © 2006 Stan Rogow Productions (U.S.), © 2006 Temple Street
Releasing Limited (Canada). Series and logo copyright © 2006 Darcy Productions
Limited, a subsidiary of Temple Street Productions Limited. DISCOVERY KIDS,
DISCOVERY and all related indicia are trademarks of Discovery Communications,
Inc., used under license. All rights reserved. DiscoveryKids.com

Published by Grosset & Dunlap, a division of Penguin Young Readers Group, 345
Hudson Street, New York, New York 10014. GROSSET & DUNLAP is a trademark
of Penguin Group (USA) Inc. Printed in the U.S.A.

Library of Congress Cataloging-in-Publication Data
Simms, Jory.   Scout's honor / by Jory Simms.
p. cm. — (Darcy's wild life ; 4)
"A Stan Rogow Book."
ISBN 0-448-44261-2
I. Title. II. Series.
PZ7.S59188Sco 2006
[Fic]—dc22   2005021687
10 9 8 7 6 5 4 3 2 1

Hi again!

I'm Sara Paxton—otherwise known as Darcy Fields on <u>Darcy's Wild Life</u>. Right now, you're holding one of two brand-new books in our <u>Darcy</u> series! And if you've noticed that we're doing things a little differently this time around, it's because we're creating new and totally original stories.

Now we can take Darcy places that the T.V. show might not be able to, opening doors for lots of new and exciting experiences. We can send Darcy on a dream vacation or bring in friends from her life back in L.A.! This time, we're sending her on a camping adventure, and we're bringing the state fair (and a cute new boy!) to Bailey. Sounds exciting, right?

So, by the time you read this book, the second season of <u>Darcy</u> will be airing. And if you're a fan of the show, you can see how much my character has been growing. Darcy was shell-shocked when her mom up and moved her to Bailey, but before long, she started getting used to the simpler life. Now, Darcy has completely bonded with her new friends (both human and animal), and she's learning so much—and loving every minute of it.

Darcy's changing a lot, too, and she's trying new things all the time. It seems like there is always an adventure just around the corner, and there are so many new and exotic animals to meet . . . Life just keeps getting wilder for Darcy, and I'm so excited to be along for the ride!

Well, I hope you're enjoying the show, and I really hope you love these books! Thanks for joining me, and happy reading!

Best Wishes!

♡ always,

Sara Paxton

Whew! Darcy here, *finally* getting a blog break in my busy day at work. Creature Comforts has been an absolute zoo lately! I know, I know—Creature Comforts is a veterinary clinic. When you work with everything from horses to hogs, you should expect things to get a little zooey. And hey, I used to live in Hollywood. I'm totally accustomed to crazy.

I'll say this much. I never get bored! One moment at the CC I might be inoculating an iguana, the next I'm massaging an arthritic mongoose. I know there was a time when just the mention of a mongoose would have freaked me out, but after months of comforting creatures, I've got to say—it's pretty fun! Animals have a way of growing on you.

The same can be said for my coworker, Lindsay. When we first met, you might remember, she was as snarly as, well, a recently inoculated iguana. But here's what I've learned—underneath all those snide comments and rolling eyes? Lindsay's a big softie and stellar friend. Lindsay's dad, Kevin, who's the veterinarian at Creature Comforts, is pretty cool, too.

Sure, sometimes I miss my old, luxe life, sipping iced chai at the Coffee Bean & Tea Leaf and buying designer clothes whenever the whim struck. I still yearn for the red carpet. And of course, I totally miss my buds back in L.A. But this whole crazy idea my mom had about ditching her movie-star ways and moving to the heartland? Well . . . maybe she was right. Our little town of Bailey has grown on me, too.

Well, folks, it's about time for me to clock out—of work and Darcy's Dish. And where am I off to? Straight home. Remember, my mom's not just a Hollywood-star-turned-farmer, she's also an Englishwoman. And that means, in addition to having a kickin' accent, she serves tea every afternoon promptly at four o'clock.

Tea is always fun. Sometimes Mom serves it iced with lots of mint and frosted cookies on the side. Sometimes we have spicy cinnamon tea and gingerbread. And lately? Mom's been going whole hog (with apologies to our pet pig, Piggy). Not only has she been breaking out the fine china, she's been baking her own scones. Clotting the clotted cream all by herself. Serving six kinds of jam and four different kinds of biscuits. (That's British for cookies, btw.) Trust me, afternoon tea at Victoria Fields's house is almost as fabulous as a mud wrap from Bliss spa. The only thing I've gotta wonder is—why is Mom working so hard to make high tea fit for a queen? After all, the only guests are usually me and Eli, our next-door neighbor/ranch hand. And maybe Lindsay's little brother, Jack, a kid who could con his way into Buckingham Palace for tea if you gave him half a chance.

Sometimes I wonder if Mom isn't feeling a little antsy. I should really do a check-in, you know, like they always do on made-for-TV movies? If only I could check in and make sure Mom's okay while *still* ensuring that the scones keep coming. Hmmm. I'll have to mull that one over on my walk home. Later!

✳   ✳   ✳   ✳   ✳   ✳

Chapter 1

Wild Wisdom . . . *Female iguanas lay their eggs in a burrow in a sunny area and leave them on their own. After the sun incubates the eggs, the baby iguanas hatch and dig their way out of the hole all by themselves.*

Darcy logged out of the Creature Comforts computer and began to gather her things. She swiped her pink marabou purse out from under the counter and dipped into it for her Juicy Tubes lip gloss. After shining up her lips, running a brush through her hair, and straightening her hot pink denim miniskirt and ruffly-but-cool Zac Posen blouse, she turned to Lindsay.

"Well, I'm off," she announced to her bud.

"Could have fooled me," Lindsay said, crossing her pale arms over her chest. "Darce, you are the only person I know who glams up to go *home* from work."

"Hey, where I'm from, you have to be camera-ready at all times," Darcy retorted with a smile. "I mean, ya never know when you're gonna be discovered.

To hear my mom talk, every old-timey movie starlet got her start at the drugstore soda fountain."

"Okay," Lindsay said. "Do you seriously think *anybody* is *ever* going to be discovered at the Dairee King in downtown Bailey?"

Darcy pictured the Dairee King, with its dusty windows and sun-bleached ads for softee cones and frozen bananas. Glam it wasn't.

"Okay, so maybe it's a stretch," Darcy said as Lindsay laughed. Darcy shrugged it off. "I guess," she admitted, "I can't get rid of my Hollywood ways any more than my mom can give up high tea. Speaking of which, her cinnamon-chip scones are calling out to me. I better motor. Ya wanna come? Sometimes Mom makes these cute little chicken salad sandwiches with no crusts. And we both *know* how much you love chicken salad."

"Not today, Malibu," Lindsay said. "Dad promised me I could feed the baby wrens this afternoon."

"You mean the baby wrens who eat only mushy cat food that you have to feed them by hand?" Darcy asked with a grin. "And you're telling me you *want* to do this? More than you want scones and chicken salad?"

"I guess it's a Bailey thing," Lindsay shrugged with a giggle. "You just wouldn't understand."

Darcy slung her fuzzy purse over her shoulder,

turned on one kitten heel, and headed for the door.

"I guess not," she laughed. "See you later, girl-friend. Give the wrens my love."

Darcy headed out the door, hopped off Creature Comforts' Wild West–style front porch, and began to saunter home. She giggled again as she passed the Dairee King on the corner of Main Street.

Not a limo or talent scout in sight, Darcy said to herself with another laugh. *Nothing but a couple of little prairie voles sprinting around the town square. Lindsay's totally right. That's Bailey for you. Instead of buying wheatgrass juice at Whole Foods, I get alfalfa at Huxton's Feed and Seed. Instead of trolling for clothes on Melrose Avenue, I've been ordering stuff online and hoping it fits. And as for night life? Well, if the Dairee King is too crowded, there's also Bailey Bowls, the 24-hour lanes. . . .*

Darcy turned off Main Street onto the gravel road that would take her home. She expertly dodged the bigger chunks of gravel that might have marred her painted toes in their strappy sandals. She crossed the road when she passed Old Man Hogsdale's exceedingly stinky cow pasture. And she grabbed a freshly fallen apple from a tree at the edge of her family's own property. She did these things almost without thinking. It wasn't until she'd turned onto her front walk that

Darcy realized that not only had she adjusted to life in Bailey, she was comfortable there!

She even . . . liked it!

I don't know whether I should be thrilled or worried, Darcy mused with a giggle. *Because I've learned something about Bailey—the minute you think you've got a handle on things here, something weird happens. And usually that something involves an animal!*

Sure enough, as Darcy approached her front door, a terrible sound made her freeze. A terrible, *beastly* sound—*coming from inside her house!*

Coo-coo-coo-Caw-caw-caw-Kaching!

The coos and caws were high-pitched and super-strident. They made Darcy cover her ears and imagine antique scary movies, the kinds about locust or bats or angry birds attacking an entire town.

Or attacking . . . her mother!

Oh no! Darcy thought. *One minute Mom's dishing up clotted cream, the next she's under attack!*

Darcy squared her shoulders and gripped the doorknob.

"Don't worry, Mom!" she called out, noticing that her own voice sounded, er, pretty worried. "I'm coming in!"

With that, Darcy plunged into the house.

Chapter 2

Wild Wisdom . . . *The bat is the only flying mammal.*

As Darcy ran through the kitchen—noticing as she dashed that there was nary a scone or strawberry in sight—she tried to imagine what horrible thing she might encounter in the next room. Would a flock of birds be pecking at her poor mother? Maybe a family of bats would be hanging from the rafters, squeaking malevolently.

Maybe it's not birds or bats, which I could totally handle, Darcy thought. She clutched her throat. *Maybe it's some kind of noisy snake, which I can totally not handle!*

The idea of a reptile invading her personal space almost made Darcy turn and run back out of the house. Only the image of her mom in trouble made her press on.

As Darcy burst into the living room, her hands covering her ears, she screamed, "*Hang on, Mom! I'm here to save* . . . uh, you?"

Darcy was stunned. Her mother was indeed in the living room, but she wasn't being tortured by madly pecking birds or predatory bats or snakes with voice boxes. She was sitting cross-legged on the floor, sur-rounded by a bunch of—little girls! It was the girls who were screeching out those *Coo-coo-coo-Caw-caw-caw-Kachings*!

As soon as Darcy stormed in, the kids' weird battle cry died down.

"Um, excuse me," piped up one of the girls. On her head, she was wearing a royal blue beanie topped with a fuzzy feather that bobbled as she talked. "But this is a highly secret meeting. Who are you?"

"I live here," Darcy retorted to the girl, who looked about nine years old. "So I think the real question is, who are *you*?"

"Darling," Victoria called out. As her mom jumped to her feet, Darcy noticed that she was wearing one of the goofy blue beanies as well. "I want to introduce you to . . . my new Jaybird Scout troop!"

"Jaybird Scouts?" Darcy squeaked, checking out the circle of grinning girls.

"Duh," said the first girl, who had glossy black

braids and a pert, upturned nose. "Didn't you recognize our Jaybird call?"

No sooner had the words left this sassy kid's mouth than all seven of the blue-beanied squirts unleashed another painful "*Coo-coo-coo-Caw-caw-caw-Kaching!*"

"Uh, thanks for the *repeat* demonstration," Darcy cringed, wiggling a finger in her ear. "What's up with that *Kaching* at the end?"

Another little girl with a mop of red curls jumped to her feet. She was clutching a blue plastic clipboard and a blue pen.

"That's because of the famous Jaybird mini muffins!" the girl explained proudly.

"The ones you guys sell door to door?" Darcy asked. *Everybody,* of course, knew about Jaybird mini muffins. Every spring, all over the country, Jaybird Scouts sold scads of them—chocolate-toffee mini muffins, blueberry-streusel mini muffins, coconut-caramel mini muffins, and Darcy's favorite, the crunchy chocolate-mint mini muffin tops. Jaybird mini muffins were totally yummy. And, apparently, profitable.

"Last year," the redheaded girl read from her clip-board, "the Jaybird Scouts sold approximately forty-four million mini muffins. Most of the profits went to environmental charities."

"Wow," Darcy said as the redhead resumed her cross-legged seat on the floor. "That's a *lot* of muffins!"

"Hence the *Kaching*," the redhead said matter-of-factly.

"I had no idea you little bluebirds were so enterprising," Darcy said, trying to stifle a smile.

"Because you were never a Jaybird Scout, Darcy," Victoria said sadly.

"Tscha," Darcy said. "I took acting lessons when I was little. Remember, Mom? Back when we were still doing that Hollywood thing?"

"Yes, and now I'm making up for lost time," Victoria burbled. "Back then, I was too busy shooting movies in exotic locations to lead a troop of Jaybird Scouts."

"Plus you had a daughter who was allergic to camping and other outdoorsy activities," Darcy pointed out, "which basically made her allergic to the Jaybird Scouts."

"There was that, too," Victoria allowed. "Anyhow, that's all in the past. Today, I'm a farmer *and* a citizen of Bailey. I thought it was about time I got involved in the town. I wanted to make a contribution to the citizens who've made us feel so welcome!"

"And your contribution is bringing a pack of Jaybirds into our home?" Darcy balked. "Mom, I think the only thing you guys are contributing to Bailey is a little noise pollution."

"Hey, that wasn't very nice," complained a skinny (but scrappy-looking) girl in the Jaybird circle. She scowled at Darcy.

"Keri, forgive my daughter," Victoria said, adjusting her blue beanie on her blond curls. "She just doesn't understand our Jaybird ways."

Suddenly Victoria clapped her hands together.

"I know," she exclaimed. "Let's conclude our meeting by showing Darcy what the Jaybirds are all about!"

"Oh, no, really," Darcy protested, trying to back out of the room. "That's okay, you guys. You carry on with your meeting, and I'll just hit the kitchen. Maybe we have some leftovers from yesterday's high tea. . . ."

"Oh, come on, sweetie," Victoria said. "It'll be fun!"

Darcy's mom had a glint in her eyes that Darcy recognized. It was her *I have a new project* glint.

I was right, Darcy thought with a sigh. *All those scones and fancy teas were a sign of boredom. And these little blue-bonneted squirts are the cure. Knowing my mom, she's going to go overboard with this troop leader thing. I guess I might as well grin and bear it—and kiss my high teas good-bye.*

17

With a sigh and a cheerful shrug, Darcy agreed to hang with the Jaybirds.

"But only on one condition," she insisted. "No more Jaybird calls! You guys could do some major eardrum damage with that thing."

"I don't get why you don't like it," protested Keri, the scrappy girl. "Whenever I go out to sell Jaybird mini muffins, I do my Jaybird call and the people love it. They buy those muffins so fast, I'm out of there in, like, seconds! I don't even have a chance to give them an encore!"

Darcy laughed.

"Excellent sales tactic, Keri," she admitted.

"True, true," Victoria piped up. "Keri's one of the Jaybirds' top mini-muffin sellers. Isn't that right, Hannah?"

The girl with the clipboard consulted her notes and nodded firmly.

"But Sophie was a close second," she said, pointing at the girl with the braids.

"Duh," Sophie said.

"I would have sold a lot, too," said a plump girl in the circle. "But, well, those muffins were so yummy. I sorta ate more than I sold."

"Girlfriend, I hear ya," Darcy said. She crossed her legs and sat next to the sheepish kid. "And what's your name?"

"I'm Ginny," the girl said. She pointed to the Jaybird sitting next to her. "This is April, my best friend."

April, who was as tall and lanky as Ginny was short and round, smiled and gave Darcy a little wave.

"And *I'm* Lizzy," piped up a blond, pigtailed girl on the other side of the circle. She slapped the back of the willowy, dark-haired girl sitting next to her and said, "And this is Alissa. And that's all of us."

"Good to meet you, Jaybirds," Darcy said with a wave. She had to admit, the girls *were* pretty cute in their beanies and blue vests covered with egg-shaped patches. "Okay, so fill me in. What are the Jaybirds all about? Besides raking in the mini-muffin bucks, that is."

"Why don't we show her?" Lizzy yelled, jumping to her feet.

"Yeah!" the other Jaybirds cried. Ginny and April began the demo by running to get some firewood from the bucket next to the fireplace.

"We have to learn how to survive in the wilderness," April said proudly. "That starts with building a camp-fire. Watch and learn."

Darcy covered her grin with her hand while April began to stack the wood in a perfect pyramid on the living room's slate floor. She nodded politely while Sophie wove a lanyard for her. Encouraged, Sophie moved on to Darcy's hair! Before Darcy could stop her, Sophie had divided her hair into many sections and started braiding up a storm.

"So . . . how does braiding hair help you survive in the wilderness?" Darcy squeaked.

Before Sophie had a chance to answer, Ginny had struck a match and held it to the base of the expertly crafted wood pyramid.

Fwooom!

The thing caught instantly.

"See?" April said proudly. "We are SO campout-ready!"

"Except we're not on a campout!" Darcy cried. "We're in the house!"

She jumped to her feet and grabbed a pitcher of Kool-Aid off the coffee table.

Luckily, the punch doused the fire. Unluckily, it left a sticky mess all over the living room floor!

"Quick thinking in a crisis, Darcy," Victoria said, nodding at the Jaybirds. "Girls, don't you think Darcy should be an honorary Jaybird?"

"Duh!" Sophie shouted enthusiastically.

"Oh, no thanks!" Darcy said, beginning to back out of the room. "As I said, I'm allergic to the wilderness. I might even have developed a sudden allergy to mini muffins! Mom, you're on your own!"

Darcy turned to flee. As she did, she slammed right into Eli, who was carrying a tray of those famous mini muffins in for the Jaybirds' snack. The muffins went flying!

"Aw, no!" Eli said. He swiped a long lock of blond-streaked hair out of his bright blue eyes.

"Sorry, Eli," Darcy said, eyeing the floor full of mini muffins. "But hey, look on the bright side. For once it was *my* klutziness that caused the spillage, not yours."

Eli was totally sweet and pretty darn cute to boot. But handy around the house he wasn't! The guy was a bona fide, if well-meaning, klutz.

Which is why he perked up when Darcy admitted her bad.

"You're right!" Eli said. "And here's another cool thing—the ten-second rule!"

He dove to scavenge the fallen muffins off the floor. Unfortunately, half of them were stuck fast!

"Um, that would be the work of some Kool-Aid," Darcy said with a cringe. "We had a little fire."

"And how do you explain those braids all over your head?" Eli wondered, his face screwed up in confusion.

Darcy rolled her eyes, but before she could answer, the braider and her cronies introduced themselves.

Well, sort of.

"Hee-hee-hee!" Several of the girls giggled behind their hands. Others pointed at Eli and whispered in each other's ears.

"Girls?" Victoria inquired. "Is there something you want to say?"

"That boy's cute!" Sophie squealed. "I should introduce him to my older sister!"

While Eli turned an alarming shade of red, Darcy shrugged and grinned at him.

"Meet Sophie," she said. "Outspoken Jaybird Scout and hair braider extraordinaire."

Eli tried to do the polite thing and say hello to Sophie and the other Scouts, but he was too embarrassed to let out more than a strangled squeak. Of course, this sent the Jaybirds into another round of shrill giggles.

Darcy grabbed Eli by the elbow and whispered to him, "If you stand still for too long, they're going to start braiding *your* hair, too!"

"Then let's make like a couple of jaybirds," Eli whispered back, "and fly outta here."

"You took the words right out of my mouth," Darcy said. "Not to mention the mini muffins. Let's go!"

Chapter 3

Wild Wisdom . . . *How much wood could a woodchuck chuck if a woodchuck could chuck wood? According to one estimate, based on the size of a typical woodchuck burrow, the answer is close to seven hundred pounds.*

The next day, Darcy woke up to a sunny day in Bailey. Make that a sunny day *off* in Bailey. It was Saturday, which meant no school and no working at Creature Comforts. As she arose from her fluffy pink bed, she thought about what to do with her day.

Darcy peeked out her open window. The air was warm and dry, with just the right amount of breeze. It would have been the perfect day for a soak in a restorative mud bath. Or a lounge by the country club pool. Or a stroll on Melrose Avenue for shopping and smoothie breaks.

If only Bailey had a country club, Darcy sighed to herself. *Or a Melrose Avenue instead of our dowdy*

*Main Street. And as for our mud? It's not really restor-
ative. It's mostly just muddy.*

Darcy might have learned to love Bailey, but she
hadn't exactly mastered finding fun stuff to do there.

Riiiinnggg.

The phone jolted Darcy out of her brood-fest.
When she answered, a breathless voice immediately
started chattering in her ear.

"Darcy! I have the best thing for us to do today! I
mean, that is, if you don't have any other plans. And
if you don't think the plan is totally lame. I mean, it's
not shopping in Beverly Hills or hanging out on your
mom's movie set or—"

"Hi, Kathi," Darcy blurted when the girl on the
other end of the line stopped to suck in a quick breath
of oxygen.

Kathi was Darcy's other steadfast Bailey bud,
and she was about as different from Lindsay as a girl
could be. Where Lindsay was dark, Kathi was sun-
shiney. While Lindsay's feet were planted firmly on
the ground, Kathi was always floating around in a
daydream. And while Lindsay liked to devote her
Saturdays to sensible things like doing homework that
wasn't due till Monday or helping her dad at Creature
Comforts, Kathi cooked up fun ideas like—

"Berry picking!" Kathi announced. "The time is ripe

for berry picking. Actually, it's the berries that are ripe!"

"Berry picking?" Darcy said with a raised eyebrow. "Well . . . that sounds . . . fun?"

"I'm so glad you think so!" Kathi said, totally not getting Darcy's major hesitation. "I kind of think of it as a treasure hunt."

"Like trawling for fabulous finds on the sale rack at Barneys," Darcy offered dreamily.

"Yeah!" Kathi agreed. "Except now, we're hunting down the plumpest, juiciest blackberries we can spot. And we have to get them *before* they're snatched off by Bailey's enormous woodchuck colony *or* by the red-breasted robins *or* by the McAllister sisters."

"The McAllister sisters?" Darcy said. She sat down at her vanity table and ran a brush through her hair. "That doesn't sound like a berry-eating animal species."

"No, they're a berry-*canning* species," Kathi explained. "The sisters are these sweet old ladies who've won the blackberry preserves contest at the last *sixteen* state fairs. They're total berry hogs. Once they've gotten to the bushes, there's hardly anything left for the rest of us! But this year, something wonderful has happened. The berries ripened early. And the McAllisters are out of town at a quilting conference! It's our chance to get some of those blackberries for ourselves, Darcy. It may be our *only* chance!"

Darcy couldn't hold her laughter back this time.

"Kathi, you are the only person I know who could make a berry-picking outing sound like a danger-packed action movie," she said.

"Does that mean you're in?" Kathi cried.

Taking another glance out into the glimmery day, Darcy grinned.

"I'm in!" she said.

"I'll bring the buckets!" Kathi announced. "See you in ten minutes!"

Plink! Plink! Plink! Plop!

"Uh-oh," Darcy said. It was an hour later and she was peering into her berry bucket in the middle of a sweet-scented thicket of bushes.

A few blackberry bushes behind her, Kathi stopped her own picking and glanced over.

"My last berry *plopped* instead of *plinked*," Darcy told her bud.

Kathi adjusted the floppy hat she was wearing to protect her pale, freckly face from the sun.

"That means it's a super-ripe one," she told Darcy. "You know what to do."

"Okay," Darcy said. She fished the berry out of her bucket and *plopped* it—right into her mouth.

"Mmmmm!" she exclaimed. "Kathi, I can't believe I ever thought that berry picking would be a bore. This fruit rocks! And I have to admit, it's fun poking through these bushes, hunting down the best berries."

"And these *are* the best berries you'll ever find," Kathi said, flipping a long auburn pigtail over her shoulder. She looked around their remote thicket of bushes at the edge of a pretty forest. "The thing about *this* blackberry patch is, nobody knows about it except me and the McAllister sisters! It's the best-kept secret in Bail—"

"All right then! Come along, girls! Everybody got their berry pails?"

Kathi froze in mid-brag. A woman's clear voice had just sounded from within the trees! And that voice had—an English accent?!?

"Mom!" Darcy squealed, looking around wildly. "Is that you?"

Suddenly, Victoria Fields—looking glam in a gauzy head scarf, a safari suit, and a galvanized tin bucket slung over one arm—broke through the trees. Trailing in her wake were seven little girls in blue beanies.

"Hey," cried Keri. "It's Darcy! Let's give her a Jaybird hello, guys!"

"No!" Darcy cried, clapping her hands to her ears.

Too late.

"Coo-coo-coo-Caw-caw-caw-Kaching!"

When the screechy sound had died away, Darcy gave Kathi a guilty look and said, "Girlfriend, meet my mom's latest project—the Jaybird Scouts, Troop Number 117."

Chapter 4

Wild Wisdom . . . *The best-known jaybird is the Canada jay, which is known for its habit of stealing bright objects. In fact, the jay is sometimes referred to as a "camp robber."*

While Kathi introduced herself to the Jaybirds, Darcy stole over to her mother.

"Mom," she whispered. "How on earth did you find this place? It's Kathi's secret blackberry stash."

"Oh, but there are plenty of berries to go around, sweetie," Victoria said. "Look at all these bushes. And did you hear that the McAllister sisters are at a quilting conference?"

"Wow, does Bailey have its own version of *Us Weekly* or something?" Darcy said. "How did you get a hold of that gossip?"

"My Jaybird Scouts, of course," Victoria quipped. "These girls are the eyes and ears of Bailey, my dear."

"Not to mention the mouths!" Darcy said. "I think as troop leader, you should make it your mission to change the Jaybird call. Or better yet, ban it altogether."

"I could never just toss out the Jaybird call!" Victoria said. "The Jaybird Scouts were founded eighty-two years ago by Mrs. Theodora Toadst."

"Toast?!" Darcy said with a chuckle. "Mrs. Toast? She should become friends with Mrs. Butterworth. They'd make a fun pair!"

"Toadst," her mother corrected her. "Darcy, you shouldn't giggle—Mrs. Toadst was a very important woman. And the first thing she did when she invented the Jaybirds was write the Jaybird call. Which means it's an American tradition."

"Yeah, but *you're* English, and *I* was never a Jaybird," Darcy said. "So it's not *our* tradition."

"Sorry, darling," Victoria said. "Even if I was going to do what you asked, I couldn't possibly fit it into today's agenda. We're going to pick loads of blackberries and then go back to our house to make jam."

"Jam?" Darcy said. She glanced over her mother's shoulder at the Jaybird Scouts, who'd quickly scattered around the blackberry bushes. They were so busy chattering and giggling that they seemed to drop one blackberry for every two they picked. Alissa and Lizzy had already gotten into a blackberry fight, and Sophie had abandoned her bucket altogether in favor of braiding Kathi's long hair.

"Um, Mom?" Darcy said. "I don't want to drag you down, but isn't jam kind of challenging for girls who can't focus on one task for more than, like, five minutes? And isn't it also *really* sticky? Might I remind you that we still haven't ungummed the living-room floor after last night's Kool-Aid incident."

"You do have a point," Victoria fretted. "But I already promised the girls we'd make jam. You see, canning food is the height of self-sufficiency. Any Jaybird who can pull it off gets a very pretty patch from the National Jaybird Adjudication Board. There's a bonus medal if you pick your own berries."

"Well, who can argue with a patch/medal double whammy," Darcy laughed. "Jam on, Mom! Have fun!"

Darcy rejoined Kathi, whose head was a tangle of braids by now.

"Ah, I remember when I was a Jaybird Scout," Kathi said, twirling one of the braids around her finger with a happy sigh. "Those were the days. I can still do a perfect Jaybird call. Wanna hear?"

"I'll give you all my blackberries if you *don't* do that Jaybird call," Darcy blurted. "In fact, I think I need a break from our little birds. They're megasweet, but they're also totally *loud*. Let's leave them these bushes and go check out that thicket over there."

Darcy pointed to a brambly bunch of bushes several yards away.

"Okay," Kathi said. "Those look like quite a challenge!"

As Darcy marched her friend past the gaggle of Jaybirds, she giggled at the berry-hurling Lizzy and Alissa. And she smiled at Ginny, who was simply eating every berry she picked. But when she saw the tiniest Jaybird—Keri—burrowing beneath a bush to grab some out-of-reach fruit, Darcy gasped.

"Watch it!" she cried, running to grab the girl's skinny elbow. She pulled Keri back before she could grab her prize.

"Hey, what gives?" Keri complained in her squeaky voice. "Everybody knows the best berries grow on the back of the bush!"

"But it looks like you *don't* know what's lurking underneath these bushes," Darcy countered. She pointed a manicured finger at the ground.

"I don't see anything!" Keri snarked. "Just some ivy or something. Big deal."

"That's *poison* ivy, dude," Darcy corrected. "*Leaves of three, let it be.* Haven't you ever heard that one?"

"Is it a pop song?" Keri blinked.

"Oh, sure," Darcy said. "It goes something like this:
Leaves of three,

let 'em be,

unless you wanna get way ITCHY!"

While Keri cackled at Darcy's impromptu ditty, Darcy's mom bounced over.

"Darcy!" she exclaimed. "I never knew you were such a nature girl."

"I'm not," Darcy admitted. "I learned that from a Saturday morning cartoon."

"Well, I'm impressed anyway," her mom declared. "What's more, you're a natural with these girls."

"Well . . ." Darcy looked down at her bucket and blushed. The truth was, she *did* kind of dig the "older and wiser" thing she had going on with these nine-year-olds.

Doing the big sister thing? And being looked up to? Darcy thought. *It definitely doesn't reek!*

"Tell you what," Victoria proposed. "When we've all gathered enough berries, I'd like you and Kathi to come home with us and help us make jam."

Darcy's eyes widened.

"Mom, are you sure?" Darcy cried. "I don't know *anything* about making jam!"

"I'm sure you know more than I do," Victoria said

with a good-natured shrug. "You *did* take home ec that one year at Beverly Hills Middle School."

"That's only because I had a crush on a boy in the home-ec class!" Darcy protested. "A crush that totally died, might I add, when we became project partners and he expected *me* to do all the work just because I'm a girl!"

"But you did learn some homemaking skills, right?" Darcy's mom said.

"I guess," Darcy said. "Let's see, I remember learning how to soft-boil an egg and grow your own herbs. And we did a whole unit on feng shui. But jam making? Sorry, Mom. That must have been part of AP home ec."

"Oh," Victoria said, biting her lip with disappointment.

"Let's face it," Darcy said, putting a hand on her mother's shoulder. "Me and Martha Stewart? *Not* separated at birth. I may make a perfect three-minute egg, but when it comes to serious cooking, I'm just not your girl."

"All right," Victoria allowed, looking despondently into her bucket. "And I'd thought that homemade blackberry preserves would make such a nice accompaniment for our Jaybird high tea."

Darcy froze.

"Did you say . . . tea?"

"Tea!" Kathi cried. "Ooh, Darcy, doesn't that sound yummy?"

Darcy looked from her pleading mother to her pleading friend to the berry-picking Jaybirds.

"Darcy," Keri piped up, "you should totally make jam with us. You're the best!"

"Duh!" Sophie shouted.

❋ (DARCY'S DISH) ❋

And *that* is how the great jam debacle began. At first, we thought it'd be easy. I mean, the recipe we found online had only three ingredients: blackberries (check), loads of sugar (check), and some stuff called pectin, which makes jelly gel.

Easy? Ha! Turns out, we were about to get ourselves into a real jam.

❋   ❋   ❋   ❋   ❋   ❋

"Okay, girls! Is everybody ready?"

Victoria was addressing her seven Scouts, who were lined up before her in the kitchen. Darcy and Kathi meanwhile were dumping bucket after bucket of blackberries into the sink for washing.

"So, here's what we're going to do," Victoria said.

"We're all going to . . . listen to Darcy!"

Darcy gasped and came dangerously close to dumping several pints of berries on the kitchen floor!

Oblivious to her distress, her mom continued. "Darcy will give us step-by-step instructions for the best blackberry jam ever!"

"Um . . . Mom?" Darcy hurried over to Victoria and whispered into her ear. "Thanks for the whole confidence thing, but did you *not* get that part about me not knowing how to make jam?"

"Yes," Victoria said casually. "But Darcy dear, all you have to do is read the steps out loud from our online recipe. Easy, peasy! Meanwhile, I'll be the adult supervisor as we handle all the piping-hot jelly jars we have to boil."

"Fiiiiinnnne," Darcy sighed, sitting at the kitchen table where her laptop was humming. She glanced at the jam recipe on the screen.

"Okay," she called over her shoulder. "The first thing you have to do is put the washed blackberries in the food processor. Then turn it on and mush 'em up. Lizzy and Alissa, why don't you take care of that?"

"Ooh, an electric appliance!" Lizzy said. "Lemme at it."

Alissa and Lizzy leaped up to the sink, their pigtails bouncing. Alissa scooped handfuls of berries out of the sink and handed them to Lizzy, who dumped them into the food processor.

"Nice cooperation, guys!" Darcy said.

"And nice leadership, Darce," her mom whispered in her ear.

Darcy couldn't help but grin. Maybe her mom knew what she was doing, making Darcy play den mom for the moment.

I'm really kinda good at this, she told herself. *Maybe after the jam, we'll even whip up some homemade peanut butt—*

Whiirrrrrrr!

"Eeeeeekkkk!"

Darcy looked up in alarm. Lizzy and Alissa were screeching—as blackberry goo spouted out of the food processor and rained stickily onto their heads!

"What did you do?!?" Darcy cried, jumping to her feet.

"I turned it on, just like you said," Lizzy wailed. Her blond hair was quickly becoming purple.

It was Victoria who saved the day, ducking through the berry shower to plunk a plastic lid onto the food-processor bowl.

"There's a *top*?" Lizzy complained, wiping fruit off her freckly cheeks. "Thanks for sharing, Darcy!"

"I guess I forgot to mention the part about putting on the top," Darcy cringed.

"No worries!" Victoria announced brightly. There are still plenty of berries to go 'round. Lizzy and Alissa, you go outside and hose yourselves down. Ginny and April, why don't you help me clean up. And Darcy, maybe you and the rest of the Jaybirds can move on to the next step."

"Okay," Darcy sighed, refocusing on her laptop screen. "This is *not* hard, guys. Let's work together here. All we have to do is boil the berries. Then add sugar and reboil for precisely one minute. Then we add pectin and boil again, while in *another* pot, we boil the jelly jars and lids, making *sure* not to boil the jam for too long. That'll make it into gelatin. And if we don't boil the berries long enough, we've got syrup. And from what it says here, if we have any pectin problems whatsoever, the jam won't gel."

Darcy looked up to a room full of Jaybirds, staring at her with open mouths.

"But other than that," Darcy blurted nervously, "it should be a breeze!"

✳ DARCY'S DISH ✳

My friends, I vow never to use the words "jam" and "breeze" in the same sentence again. And I think I've sworn off PB and Js for a while, too. . . .

✳ ✳ ✳ ✳ ✳ ✳

Chapter 5

Wild Wisdom . . . *Goats do not have any upper front teeth.*

"Oh, man," Lindsay said the next day at Creature Comforts. Darcy was filling her in on the Great Blackberry Jam Jam. Between bouts of hysterical laughter, Lindsay was drilling her for more information. "So after the blackberry shower, you guys finally started cooking?"

"Ugh, yeah," Darcy recalled. She'd snagged a black kitten out of the clinic and was cuddling it as she told her story.

"Hannah was all into stirring and tasting and stirring and tasting," Darcy went on, "to make sure the jam was just right—not too sweet and not too sour."

"Oh yeah, I know Hannah," Lindsay nodded. "Very meticulous. She brings her Lhasa apso into Creature Comforts like every other week for a full bath and grooming."

"Yeah, well *after* all that tasting?" Darcy said.

"Hannah spotted a worm floating in the jam pot!"

"Blackberries come from the wild," Lindsay said sagely. "Worms happen."

"Yeah, well, Hannah freaked," Darcy sighed. "She threw the worm across the room, where it landed on—"

"Don't say it!" Lindsay cried, bursting into laughter again.

"Me!" Darcy wailed. "And lemme tell ya, worms and I? We don't get along so well either."

"So then what happened?" Lindsay rasped. She was laughing so hard, she tipped over the pyramid of hamster-food cans that she'd just stacked on the counter.

"Well, I kinda freaked, too, and knocked the sugar onto the floor," Darcy said.

"Oh, man," Lindsay said again. "How much sugar?"

"About ten pounds," Darcy cried. "Do you know how hard it is to clean up ten pounds of spilled sugar? The Jaybirds tracked it through the whole house, of course. I crunch every time I take a step!"

"Aw, isn't that sweet?" Lindsay cooed.

"Ha, ha," Darcy said drily.

"No, I mean it," Lindsay said, pointing to the kitten in Darcy's arms. "Look!"

Darcy looked down to see the squirmy black kitty licking her arm as if it were a lollipop.

"It's the sugar!" Darcy complained, putting the kitten down to scamper around the floor. "I feel like a giant frosted flake."

"Aw, don't cry over spilled sugar," Lindsay joked. "At least that was the worst of it."

"Oh no," Darcy said. "I haven't even gotten to the part where we asked Eli to go to the store and get replacement sugar."

"Uh-oh," Lindsay said. Like everyone else in Bailey, Lindsay knew all about Eli's notorious klutziness.

"Yup," Darcy said. "Spillage number two. Followed by a major titter-fest from the Jaybirds."

"Were they hyper from too much sugar?" Lindsay said.

"No, boy crazy for Eli!" Darcy said. "They were giggling so hard, they missed half my instructions for the jam."

"And the moral of the story is?"

"Let's just say it's too bad the Jaybirds don't sell pancakes instead of mini muffins," Darcy said. "Because we've got a vat of blackberry syrup on our hands."

"Ungelled jelly," Lindsay said, shaking her head in mock sorrow. "Well, the McAllister sisters will be glad to know their winning streak is safe."

"Winning streak? Now you're talking my language! Wassup, ladies!"

Darcy and Lindsay looked at each other and rolled

their eyes. Then they crossed their arms wearily over their chests and turned to face the short and skinny kid sauntering through the door.

"Hi, Jack," they droned together.

"Forget the niceties," Jack said. "Let's get right to the meat of the matter. Winning streak. Now, are we talking lotto? Or the Waffle Hut daily trivia question? Or video blackjack? Whatever it is, deal me in. I'm a broke man."

"Man?!" Darcy sputtered. "You're ten!"

"And does that mean I have no rights?" Jack protested, stomping one sneakered foot. "I may be a kid, but I have a right to life, liberty, and the pursuit of happiness. Which, in my case, means the pursuit of a bigger allowance!"

❋ DARCY'S DISH ❋

You remember Jack Adams, don't you? He's Lindsay's little brother *and* Bailey's very own resident con artist. Come up with any scheme and Jack's come up with it first. The little dude has one dream and one dream only—to make it to Hollywood. When he first met my mom, he was sure that she was his ticket to Cali. But after months of Jack begging and Mom no-ing, Jack's pretty much convinced that Mom's quit Hollywood for good.

So his latest "Get to Beverly Hills Quick" scheme? In Jack's own words: "Hey, not everybody's rich and famous in Hollywood. Some people are just rich. And I intend to be one of those people."

So far, Jack has attempted to make money with a "Name Your Farm Animal" service—until he found out that my mom was the only farmer in Bailey who cared to name her animals. Then Jack put flyers all over town declaring himself a punk animal groomer. He forgot that most goats already have cool goatees and most pigs have fabulous sticky-uppy bristles without the help of hair gel. Jack's Barnyard Barber Shop barely got off the ground.

But is Jack discouraged? No way. The kid is always lurking about, looking for his next scheme. Too bad he's hit a dead end with us.

❄   ❄   ❄   ❄   ❄   ❄

"Dream on," Lindsay sputtered to her sullen little brother. "Dad is *so* not raising your allowance. You hardly do any work around here!"

"Hey!" Jack said, pointing a squat finger at Lindsay. "Did I or did I not fetch a drink of water for Mr. Perkins just this morning?"

Jack pointed at the old man who took up a permanent spot on a bench near Creature Comforts' front door. The old coot spent his life napping in the shop, so Darcy had taken to calling him Snoozie. She called the pet mouse that lived in Mr. Perkins's hat Coco, after her favorite fashion designer, Coco Chanel.

And she called Jack . . . a pretty nice kid for helping to hydrate old Snoozie.

Maybe, Darcy told herself, *Jack's not as smarmy as I thought—*

"You only brought Mr. Perkins water so you could search through his pockets for spare change!" Lindsay accused. "Don't think I didn't see that, Jack!"

"I was just looking for a little rightful compensation," Jack protested. "A quarter for a big cup of water is a very fair price."

While Lindsay huffed in frustration, Darcy said, "And to think I used to beg my mom for a little brother. What was I thinking?"

Jack stuck his tongue out at Darcy and plopped onto the floor to play with the black kitten, while Lindsay squinted at Darcy.

"So maybe instead you'd like a little sister?" Lindsay asked. "One with a blue beanie?"

"Hello?" Darcy said. "Have I not spent the last hour telling you about the Jaybird-induced mayhem at *Château Fields*?"

"Yeah," Lindsay said, "but you've *also* been telling me how Sophie's all attitudinal and cool. And how Hannah's totally going to be a CEO someday. And how Alissa is too pretty for words. Face it, you're a total den mom. You've even learned how to use a food processor!"

"Whatever," Darcy said, leaning against the counter. "Can I help it if the girls look up to me? I mean, I *am* fifteen. It's sorta my civic duty to impart wisdom and understanding to the younger generation."

Now it was Lindsay and Jack who rolled their eyes at each other.

"Hey, I saw that," Darcy said.

"Of course you did," Jack said. "Being so *old* and *wise* and all, you don't miss a thing."

"Ha, ha," Darcy said. "Being old means I *also* have work to do, squirt. So maybe you could keep it down while I call tomorrow's patients to confirm their appointments."

Jack bowed deeply.

"Aged wise one," he intoned. "Be my guest."

Darcy shot a teasing scowl at Jack and reached for the phone. Just before she picked it up, it rang!

"That's funny," Darcy said as she grabbed the phone. "Hello? Creature Comforts."

"Darcy, is that you?"

"Mom!" Darcy said. "Don't tell me you're calling to say that the sugar has made its way upstairs. You know I can't sleep a wink if I've got gritty sheets."

"Oh, don't worry about the sugar, darling," Victoria said. "A colony of ants has come to our rescue. They've been zipping in and out of the kitchen all morning, snatching up the grains that we missed."

"Ants?" Darcy blurted. "Well, I guess those are *slightly* less gross than worms."

"Darcy," Victoria said, "ants are very industrious creatures and not gross at *all*. In fact, they've given me a fabulous idea."

Darcy bit her lip and braced herself. Victoria's fabulous ideas could be scary!

"I think my Jaybird troop should go on a nature hike," Victoria declared.

"An *outdoor* activity," Darcy replied with a sigh of relief. "Mom, I think that's a stellar idea. You *should* go on a hi—"

"But not just a hike," Victoria said. "I'm thinking— an overnight camping trip! The girls could practice their survival skills and their tent-pitching prowess. And there are oodles of opportunities for patches and medals on an overnight."

"Well, I'm sure I could stay with Lindsay or Kathi while you're gone," Darcy said encouragingly. "We'll have our *own* kind of overnight. If only they gave out patches for making avocado facial masks, painting your toenails, or watching Orlando Bloom movies."

"No, Darcy, you don't understand," Victoria said. "I called because I want *you* to come with us!"

"Me?!" Darcy gasped. "Mom! I don't know anything about camping."

"Neither do I," Victoria chirped. "Which is why we both need to go on this trip. We live in the country now. We need to develop our outdoor skills. I think it would be an excellent example to the Jaybirds if they could see us learning alongside them."

"Hi, Mrs. Fields? Jack Adams here, coming at ya from the other extension."

Darcy jumped as Jack's voice rasped both in her ear and next to her. The kid had clearly gotten the gist of Darcy's conversation and picked up Creature Comforts' second phone. He smirked at Darcy as he spoke to Victoria.

"I think a camping trip is an excellent idea," Jack said. "Darcy was just telling me how much she enjoys imparting wisdom to today's youth."

"Well said, Jack," Victoria cried. "So, Darcy, it's settled, then? I've already gotten us a couple of enormous backpacks at the hardware store in town. When you get home from work, we'll start packing!"

Chapter 6

Wild Wisdom . . . *Bear cubs are usually born as twins.*

Darcy hung up the phone and whirled to stare Jack down.

"So," Jack said nervously, "you're going on a trip, huh? That's great!"

"Oh yeah, really great," Darcy replied sarcastically as she took a few threatening steps toward the squirt. "And I have you to thank for it!"

"Now, Darcy, just calm down," Jack said as he backed away slowly. "I thought you'd *like* going camping."

"Really?" Darcy quipped. "Because *I* thought you'd like a noogie!"

With her knuckles raised and aimed at Jack's shaggy head, Darcy began to chase the kid around the Creature Comforts counter.

"Hey!" Jack shrieked. "Violence isn't the answer. Especially when I was just trying to do you a favor!"

"Some favor!" Darcy said, slowing down. "Do you realize that because of you I'm going to have to sleep *on the ground*? I'm going to have to hike miles and miles? And will I get a nice hot shower afterward? Oh no. I'll get a cold bath in some icky pond! So Jack, I'm wondering how on *earth* you thought this was a favor to me?"

"It's a vacation!" Jack cried. "A chance to get away. From your house. Which I hear is totally encrusted in sugar and blackberries and stuff."

"He does have a point," Lindsay piped up from behind Darcy. "By the time you and your mom get back, Eli should have everything cleaned up."

Darcy got a squinty, scheming look on her face as she turned to her friend.

"You mean, by the time *we* get back?" she said to Lindsay.

"Um, excuse me?" Lindsay choked out. "Did you say 'we'?"

"As in you and me!" Darcy told her. "Please, Lindsay? Come with me. If you don't, I might die!"

"How? Death by s'more?" Lindsay scoffed. "No way am I going camping with you. I mean, I like camping as much as the next girl—"

When she saw Darcy's baleful look, Lindsay added, "—well, the next Bailey girl anyway. What I *don't* like is being braided into oblivion by a bunch of Jaybird Scouts. I've got enough to deal with being big sister to Jack-rabbit over there."

"Hey!" Jack said, stomping his foot again. He stomped so hard, in fact, that he bounced several inches into the air.

"I rest my case," Lindsay said before she and Darcy both collapsed into giggles. In the midst of her laughter, Darcy saw Jack starting to slip out the door.

"Hey," she yelled after him. "I may be laughing, but I'm still mad. I totally blame you for this camping trip!"

Jack twisted around and gave Darcy a desperate look.

"But you *are* still going, right?" he said. "You and your mom *are* leaving town for two days?"

"I guess so," Darcy grumbled. "Mom's really psyched about this, and I hate to disappoint her."

"Yes!" Jack said, pumping his fist. "That's all I needed to know. See ya, Darce! Watch out for bears out there!"

"Bears?!" Darcy screamed as Jack scampered away. She whirled around to face Lindsay. "He's kidding, right?"

"I take the Fifth," Lindsay laughed.

❋ (DARCY'S DISH) ❋

I was just on the verge of a major freak-out when
Kathi walked in with her cute pug, Skittles. Skittles is
mad for the free dog biscuits we give out at Creature
Comforts. He drags Kathi in for a nosh every chance
he gets.

❋   ❋   ❋   ❋   ❋   ❋

"Kathi!" Darcy screeched. "*You'll* save me. I have
to go on an overnight trip with the Jaybird Scouts,
and Lindsay *refuses* to go with me!"

"And we segue into *Drama Queen, Part Two*,
starring Darcy Fields," Lindsay muttered.

Meanwhile, Kathi was her usual amped self.

"A camping trip!" she cried. "Far out."

"I guess it's far out," Darcy shrugged. "Maybe a
few hours away. Mom didn't say."

"No," Kathi blurted. "I meant, cool! I loooove
camping."

"Why does that not surprise me, Miss Berry
Picker," Darcy said with a smile. "So you'll go with
me?"

"Totally," Kathi said. "I mean, I have to ask my
parents. But if they're in, *I'm* in."

Kathi grabbed a biscuit from the free-biscuit bowl
and fed it to her bug-eyed little dog, Skittles.

"This trip'll be so fun, Darcy," she said happily. "I mean, how exciting to pitch your own tent to protect you from the elements. To break out a water purifying kit whenever you're thirsty. To have to build a fire whenever you're hungry. It really puts life in perspective for you."

"Like, it sort of makes you realize how much you love electricity and plumbing and microwave ovens and stuff?" Darcy said.

"I was thinking more of not sweating the small stuff and appreciating the simple life," Kathi replied.

Darcy slumped against the counter.

"Okay, *that* sounds scary," Darcy joked.

A moment later, though, she got serious again. She cast a sad glance at her friends.

"Lindsay, I want you to know that if I don't return from this treacherous trip, you can have my iPod. And Kathi, my lip-gloss collection is yours."

"Oh, please," Lindsay sputtered. "That's the most pathetic thing I've ever heard. You've made your point, Darcy. I'll go, too!"

"Really!?" Darcy cried. She jumped up and down, then slung her arms around both her friends' shoulders.

"You guys are the best," she cried. "With you at my side, I can completely handle this camping thing."

Chapter 7

Wild Wisdom . . . *The two-toed sloth spends almost its entire life upside down—eating, sleeping, and even giving birth.*

"Okay, I really cannot handle this camping thing." Darcy sighed.

She was sitting on her bed that night, looking at the enormous pile of supplies she'd laid out for the trip and the puckery red backpack her mother had given her.

"Mom," Darcy called through her open door. "I thought you said this backpack was enormous!"

"It's the biggest one they had!" Victoria called back. "Really, Darcy, we're going rustic! You shouldn't need more than a pair of clean underwear and a toothbrush, with environmentally friendly toothpaste, of course!"

Darcy gasped in horror.

Maybe Mom can rough it, she told herself. *I mean she did survive that notoriously tough movie shoot in*

Nepal for her blockbuster Ever My Everest. *But I am not an eccentric movie star, and I need provisions. I'm sure my buds will back me up.*

Darcy grabbed her laptop and started typing. . . .

❊ ⟨ **DARCY'S DISH** ⟩ ❊

Guys, I ask you: Would you be caught in the wilderness without a full arsenal of attire? I mean, suppose you're wading through a cold river? Capris, am I right? They keep your knees warm while your toes take a bath. And for a hike in full sun? Shorts, halter top, and a floppy hat to protect you from the harsh rays. Then again, you never know when mosquitoes or a cold snap might hit, and that's why I need jeans—distressed for a casual daytime look and dark denim for nighttime. Just because you're sitting around a campfire doesn't mean you can't be fashion-forward. . . .

❊   ❊   ❊   ❊   ❊   ❊

As Darcy blogged on (and on and on) about the logic behind her to-pack list, her mother poked her head through her bedroom door.

"My, my, but that's a big pile," she said, looking at the clothes, makeup, and other gear heaped onto Darcy's bed. "I've already finished packing. I hardly

needed a thing because I found these brilliant pants at
the sporting-goods store. They're convertible!"

She held a pair of drab khakis out for Darcy to
see. Darcy gasped. The pants were too ugly for words!

"You see, now they're pants," Victoria said.

Darcy nodded weakly.

"But now . . ." Victoria reached down and tugged
at a zipper on one of the pant legs. ". . . it's a pair of
shorts!" she exclaimed as the bottom of the pant leg
fell to the floor.

Darcy covered her mouth with her hands.

"Mom," she squeaked, "what's happened to you?
You used to have Karl Lagerfeld on your speed dial.
And now you're wearing convertible pants?!"

"I think they're quite clever, actually," Victoria
said, smiling down at her new pants. "They're all you
need to survive during an overnight."

"But, but," Darcy protested, "they have gathered
ankles. And they're made of icky polyester. Worst of
all is that waistband! It's . . ." Darcy's voice dropped
to a whisper. ". . . elastic! Mom, if the tabloids saw
you in those pants, they'd be all over you. You'd be
the Fashion Don't of the week!"

"That's the point of going on a camping trip,"
Victoria laughed. "We're getting away from those

kinds of worries. The only makeup I'm bringing is a bottle of sunscreen and a smile. I think you should do the same, sweetie."

"Uh-huh," Darcy said dubiously.

"Oh, and don't forget this little item," her mom said as she turned to leave Darcy's room. She pulled something out of her pocket and tossed it over. Darcy caught it before she could ID it.

"It's a camping must-have!" Victoria said before heading for her own bedroom. "Night-night!"

Darcy looked at the heavy item in her hand.

It had two handles, a sharp little wheel, and a twisty knob. It took Darcy a full ten seconds to figure out what it was. And when she did, a new wave of horror washed over her.

"A non-electric can opener?!" she cried. "You mean I'm going to have to eat food out of cans?! Ack!!!"

The next morning, Darcy awoke at dawn. She *didn't* want to wake at dawn, of course, but she had no choice, what with the bugle revelry blaring through the house! Not to mention her mother poking her cheerful head into her bedroom.

"Up and at 'em!" Victoria shouted over the bugle blasts. "We've got a big day ahead of us, Darcy!"

"Does that also include a big breakfast?" Darcy said hopefully as she slumped out of bed.

Her mother tossed her an energy bar. Darcy rubbed the sleep out of her eyes and squinted at the label.

"Whole grains?" she squawked. "Soy protein? Mom, this is *so* not a waffle with a side of scrambled eggs."

"But it *is* quick!" Victoria said cheerfully. "Hup, hup, darling. Downstairs in five."

"Ma'am, yes, ma'am," Darcy said, saluting her mom like a marine.

After throwing on her carefully chosen traveling outfit (drawstring linen pants and a sporty-yet-feminine lilac tank top), Darcy dragged her backpack downstairs.

When she shuffled into the kitchen, she was surprised to find her boss, Kevin, standing next to Eli at the counter. Eli looked as bleary as Darcy felt, but Kevin was scrubbed, combed, and chipper.

This being cheerful in the a.m. must be an adult thing, Darcy thought.

"Morning, Darcy!" Kevin said. "I was just telling your mom that your van is ready to go!"

He pointed into the pantry, where Victoria was busy loading her backpack with nonperishable provisions.

"We're using your van?" Darcy said. "The one you use to transport dogs and pigs?"

"And don't forget goats and sheep," Kevin said. "One time I even gave a sloth a lift. The little guy dug his claws into the upholstery and wouldn't let go. Far too many people underestimate the stubbornness of sloths."

Kevin shook his head and laughed.

"Um, Kevin, I don't mean to be rude, but you know all those animals you cart around in your van?" Darcy said. "They have just a little bit of an . . . odor to them. Not that there's anything wrong with that. If you're a veterinarian, that is."

Darcy shuffled uncomfortably while Kevin smiled at her cluelessly.

"I'm just thinking of the Jaybird Scouts," she added. "You know how fussy nine-year-olds can be about strange smells."

"Well, Darcy, I was a dad once," Kevin said. "Still am, in fact."

He pointed at the kitchen table where Lindsay was gnawing her own energy bar and where Jack was fast asleep, his shaggy head resting on his folded arms.

"So I *did* think about the smelly factor," Kevin continued. "And that's why I brought you this!"

Kevin pulled a little cardboard pine tree out of his pocket and proudly presented it to Darcy.

"It's an air freshener," he announced. "You hang it on the rearview mirror—a pleasure to the eyes *and* the nose."

"Great." Darcy sighed. "Thanks, Kevin."

"You should also thank him," Victoria said as she emerged from the pantry, "for holding down the fort for us while we're gone."

"Yup!" Kevin said. He clapped Eli on the back. "Eli and I are going to make sure your horse is fed, your goats are milked, and your pig pen is nice and muddy. You don't have to worry about your farm while *we're* on the case."

"That sounds like a lot of work," Darcy said slyly. "Hey . . . maybe I should stay home so I can help you!"

"As if!" Lindsay said. She'd finished her energy bar and jumped up from the kitchen table. "If I'm going on this Jaybird thing, *you're* going."

"And we're *going* right now!" Victoria announced. "Come on, girls. Let's pile into the van and go pick up our Jaybirds."

Clutching her pine-tree air freshener for dear life, Darcy waved good-bye to Kevin, Eli, and the sleeping Jack and walked sadly out the door.

❋ ⟨ **DARCY'S DISH** ⟩ ❋

Hello, everyone. And good-bye! The cell-phone towers in the wilderness are few and far between, so this could be my last blog for a while. From here on out, I'll just write in my travel journal with a pen. It's primitive, but it'll have to do. Now, some final words before I sign off: If I don't survive, my iPod and my lip-gloss collection are already spoken for, but the rest of you can divide up my clothes among yourselves. As for my CDs and DVDs, well—

❋　　❋　　❋　　❋　　❋　　❋

Blip!

Darcy stared at the screen of her PDA, her mouth hanging open.

OUT OF RANGE. TRANSMISSION INTERRUPTED.

Sure enough, when Darcy looked up, she realized that her mom had driven their superlong van—brimming with Darcy, Kathi, Lindsay, seven squirming Jaybirds, and a whole lot of backpacks—onto a winding, wooded road.

So it's happened, Darcy thought with a shuddery sigh. *We've crossed the line from civilization to wilderness. I just hope my mom can maintain control of the sitch.*

"Um . . ." said Victoria, looking a lot more uncertain than a van driver should look. "Does anyone happen to know if we've passed Gilmore Drive?"

"Sorry, I was blogging, so I wasn't paying attention," Darcy said. "I bet Lindsay was. She's always on top of things."

Darcy turned in her seat to look back at Lindsay, who was squeezed in the middle of four Jaybirds. Her hair was being twisted into about a dozen braids, several of which hung over her eyes.

"Huh?" she said. "I can't see a thing back here. I'm being braided to death."

"We can smell, though!" Sophie said as she coolly continued weaving Lindsay's hair. "Pine trees plus poodles—pee-ew!"

Darcy huffed and turned back to her mom.

"Are you saying we're lost, Mom?" she said.

"Well, in a manner of speaking," Victoria said breezily, "we are lost. But you could also say we've found an opportunity!"

She raised her voice and called back to the Jaybird Scouts.

"Girls," she said. "Did you know that there's a Jaybird badge for map-reading skills?"

Chapter 8

Wild Wisdom . . . *Ferrets sleep eighteen hours a day. They're usually active around dusk, and they have very poor eyesight.*

Back at the ranch, Eli was feeling *pret-ty* proud of himself. While Kevin had spent the morning checking up on all the animals, Eli had gathered eggs from the chicken house and weeded Victoria's vegetable garden. He'd mowed the front lawn and repaired a cracked shutter on the farmhouse window. Then he'd made lunch for himself and Kevin and Jack.

But that wasn't what made Eli proud. As Victoria's right-hand farmhand, he did these kind of chores every day. *Usually,* however, his chores were accompanied by a host of accidents. He was famous for *dropping* half the eggs he gathered, for instance. Or hauling a bag of pig feed all the way from the barn to the pigpen before he noticed a hole in the feed bag. Or splitting that cracked shutter in two instead of nailing it together.

But today, Eli had been error-free! The eggs were intact. The pigs were fed. The shutter was whole and hung perfectly straight.

Eli was so happy, he wanted to do a little celebratory jig. But he was afraid he'd knock into something and break it if he did. Instead, he just (carefully) washed the lunch dishes and sauntered out of the house with a big smile on his face.

Kevin strolled along behind him, while Jack scampered off to play behind the house.

"So, Dr. Adams," Eli said, "that was a pretty productive morning, eh? And accident-free, I might add."

"Y'know, I hadn't noticed it," Kevin said, "but you're right. I guess you *are* kind of accident-prone, huh, Eli?"

"Yeah," Eli said, hanging his head gloomily.

"No worries," Kevin said, clapping his young friend on the back. "When I was a teenager like you, I was as klutzy as they come!"

"Really?" Eli said, his sun-burnished face brightening.

"Oh, sure," Kevin said. "It goes along with the growth spurt, the voice change, the dreaming about junk food all day. It's a puberty thing."

"So, you're saying, I won't be like this forever?" Eli said hopefully.

"Yup," Kevin said. "Just look at me. The other day, I did major surgery on a ferret, and the little guy made it through with flying colors. Look."

The vet held out his hands. Eli leaned over to peer at them carefully.

"Yup!" he said, raising his thick eyebrows. "Not a tremble."

"That'll be you some day," Kevin said. "As for now, well, I guess we'll have to wait and see if your klutzy days are over or if this peaceful morning was just a fluke."

"And if it was?" Eli said fearfully.

"Well," Kevin said, glancing at his watch. "We've spent the last four minutes talking about this. I'd say that's a pretty big jinx, wouldn't you?"

"Aw, no!" Eli cried, slapping a hand to his forehead.

"Don't worry," Kevin said. "The last task on our to-do list is a cinch. Can you walk with me to the Brennan brothers' ranch?"

"Oh, I don't know," Eli said, slumping to sit on the house's front steps. "The last time I went over there, a giraffe almost tripped over me! And remember the time before that? When you asked me to pick up that family of hedgehogs for you?"

"Ouch," Kevin recalled with a wince. "All those quills must have hurt! You're right, Eli. When you go to the Brennans, you never know what you're gonna get. Those guys have rehabilitated every exotic animal I can think of. You know, of course, about their llama, Oprah. But there are also anteaters, antelopes, aardvarks, Abyssinian cats. And under the *B's* . . ."

"Um, I get the picture, Dr. Adams," Eli said, holding up his hands. "So what kind of crazy critter are you picking up from them today?"

"Not picking up," Kevin corrected his sidekick. "Delivering."

He motioned for Eli to follow him to the barn. In the cool, hay-scented building, Kevin pointed at a small animal crate on the dirt floor.

"Y'see, since I loaned my van to the Jaybird troop, the only way I can deliver these critters is on foot," Kevin said. "That's where you can help me, Eli. It's just a bit too big for me to carry myself, but with two of us on the case, the walk will be easy."

"Well . . ." Eli said dubiously. "What's in there?"

"Just a couple of prairie voles," Kevin shrugged. "They're no bigger than chipmunks."

"Prairie voles?" Eli said. He dropped to his hands and knees to peek through the crate's mesh door. Inside he saw two little grayish brown rodents, curled around each other.

"Awwwww," Eli said. "They're cute! Why're these little guys going to the Brennans? Are they injured?"

"Quite the opposite," Kevin said. "Eli, are you familiar with the prairie vole?"

"No," Eli said. He stood back up and looked at the vet.

"These voles are famous for being monogamous," Kevin said.

"Ooh!" Eli said. "That does sound scary— whatever it means."

Kevin laughed.

"It means that they have one mate and one mate only," he explained. "When prairie voles get hitched, they stay married for life."

"Oh!" Eli said, nodding. "Well, that's kind of nice, isn't it?"

"Sure," Kevin said. "There's just one problem, though. When Mrs. Prairie Vole gets in a family way, her husband gets *very* protective."

"Oh," Eli said. He thought for a moment and then exclaimed, "Oh! So you mean one of those little voles—"

"Is expecting even littler voles," Kevin confirmed. "And her male mate is awfully protective of her. So much that he's been wreaking havoc all over Bailey. He's stolen nuts and berries from the Bailey-Wick Market. He's dug up every vegetable garden he can find. And he's been pouncing on anyone who stumbles upon the voles' nest, which is unfortunately located smack-dab in the middle of the town square.

"Mrs. Vole's pregnancy has become inconvenient for all of us," Kevin went on. "So I thought it'd be a good idea if these guys took a little vacation at the Brennans until their babies arrive. After the offspring grow up, Mr. Vole should be back to his friendly self."

"That sounds reasonable," Eli said, dusting off his hands. "And all you need me to do is help you carry the crate to the Brennans?"

"That's all," Kevin said. "It's about a mile away. Can you handle it?"

Eli thought again.

"What about the jinx?" he asked.

"Well, that all depends on whether you believe in jinxes," Kevin offered.

Just like a dad, Eli thought, *to leave the decision-making up to me. Okay, here's the deal. If we make it to the Brennans without a disaster, then maybe I can declare my klutz curse lifted! And if we don't—what's the big*

67

deal? It's just a couple of prairie voles. We'll recatch 'em and get them to the Brennans anyway.

"Dr. Adams," Eli declared, puffing out his chest with confidence, "I'll do it. Let's go!"

The man and boy bent down and swooped up the crate. It was pretty big, but very lightweight.

See, Eli told himself as he and Kevin carried the crate out of the barn. *This is going to be a bree—*

"*Bleeeet!*"

Eli jumped as the crate began rocking and rolling in his hands. The cozy-looking prairie voles had clearly been jolted out of their cuddle, and they were *not* happy about it.

"Whoa," Eli said as he struggled to maintain his grasp on his end of the crate. "Prairie voles are more powerful than they look."

"Especially when they're being territorial," Kevin said with a nod. "You wouldn't believe how mad they were when I trapped them using the prairie voles' favorite food—grass smeared with peanut butter. This little guy is smart. He's not going to let that happen again!"

"Really?!" Eli said, feeling his knees suddenly go shaky. "You know, Dr. Adams? Maybe this wasn't such a good idea after all. I don't want to mess up a high-stakes mission."

"Nonsense," Kevin declared. "I trust you, Eli! Besides, there's nobody else here to help me, and I really need to transport these voles."

Okay, I think that was a vote of confidence, Eli thought.

He gritted his teeth and steeled himself as they made their way across the yard.

"*Bleeeet! Bleeet! Bleeet!*"

"Whoa, the little guy is *not* happy, huh?" Eli said.

"Just keep it slow and steady, and we'll make it," Kevin said.

"Right," Eli said. "Slow and steady, slow and stead-yyyyy!"

Eli had just stepped on something. Something very slippery! Before he knew it, he was crashing to the ground, and the prairie-vole crate was flying from his hands!

"Aw, no!" he cried as he and the crate hit the dirt at the same time. The crate's little door flew open and the fuzzy brown voles shot outside. Being voles, which are happiest burrowed away from the outside world, they raced for the first shelter they spotted—the house! The kitchen door just happened to be wide open.

"The voles!" Kevin cried.

"Curses!" Eli shouted. "Literally! My klutziness is *so* not cured."

As he pushed up from the ground, his hand touched something slimy.

"Huh?" he said, lifting it out of the dirt. "It's a wrapper from a stick of butter! This must be from all the scones Victoria's been making lately. But how did it get here? Right in my path? Making me fall and ruin everything!?!"

"Did you say you had a butter wrapper?"

Eli looked up blearily. That was Jack, hurrying over to Eli, lugging a big, smelly garbage bag behind him.

"Sorry, dude," Jack said, swiping the slimy wrapper out of Eli's hand. "I must have dropped that. I was, er, trying to help by taking out the garbage! Yeah, and the butter wrapper must have fallen out."

"And when I had the entire barnyard to choose from," Eli groaned, "*that's* where I put my big, clumsy foot. Great."

While Jack shrugged guiltily and trotted away, Eli peeked up at Kevin.

"Sorry, sir!" he said. "I'll do everything I can to help you find the voles."

"And we'd better find them soon," Kevin said. "We've got a pregnant vole and her mad-as-heck mate in the house! They could tear the place apart!"

Chapter 9

Wild Wisdom . . . *Owls can't move their eyes. Instead, they have to turn their heads to see up, down, and to the side. Luckily, they can turn their heads 180 degrees.*

DARCY'S TRAVEL JOURNAL

Shocking but true—we actually made it. But for a while there, our Scout troop was loster than lost. Trying to get ourselves found went something like this:

ME: "If we could just get ourselves within range of a satellite feed, I could use the global positioning system on my PDA to figure out where we are."

KERI: "That's cheating! The Jaybird Scouts read maps. Or we use the North Star to find our way."

ME: "Keri, it's eight-thirty in the morning. We've got about twelve hours before we get a glimpse of the North Star. But in mere minutes, I could call AAA with my cell and get some help."

HANNAH: "Excuse me, Darcy, but I've consulted my

Jaybird rule book, and there is no badge or medal awarded for cell phoning."

And so on and so forth. But finally, the girls saved the day in a totally Jaybird-sanctioned way! Ginny and April read a map! (As soon as they figured out which end of the map was up, that is.) They put us on track and scored themselves a couple of Geographic Orientation badges. Unfortunately, all that map reading made April vansick— which led to everybody telling their favorite throw-up stories for the rest of the ride.

Let's just say, the word "gross" doesn't begin to cover it. When we finally reached our destination, I kissed the ground in gratitude!

(Okay, I did not *actually* kiss the ground. Dirt and lip gloss do not mix. But in my *head*, I kissed the ground.) Little did I know that our van ride had been a walk in the park compared to what lay ahead—a much, er, *harder* walk in the park.

❋   ❋   ❋   ❋   ❋   ❋

"Here we are, girls," Victoria announced, hopping cheerfully out of the van. "The Roaming Bear National Park."

"Which," Darcy told the young Scouts reassuringly, "is just a picturesque image and not an actual representation of the park's inhabitants."

Then she turned to Lindsay and whispered in her ear, "Right? I'm right, aren't I? There aren't really roaming bears here?"

Lindsay smiled her sly smile and said cryptically, "You know what's funny? We always think about wild animals crowding our personal space, when really it's us invading their space. I mean, who was here first, really? Us or them?"

"Okay, Lindsay?" Darcy whispered. "Somehow I'm less than reassured."

"Well, then you should ask Kathi about her uncle Lyle," Lindsay suggested. "He was attacked by a bear and he totally survived. With almost all of his fingers! It's a really reassuring story."

"Yeah, really," Darcy said in a tremulous voice as she slumped to the back of the van. The Jaybirds dug out their backpacks, most of which were pink and purple and adorably small. Kathi's, too, was pea green and featherlight.

"Wow," Darcy said, handing Kathi her backpack. "This must be made of some high-tech fabric—it doesn't weigh a thing!"

"Well, all I packed was a change of T-shirt and some dry socks," Kathi shrugged. "It's just an overnight."

"Oh," Darcy said, biting her lip.

Her mother had just pulled the last of the Scouts' packs from the back of the van and was getting ready to slam the door closed.

"Um, Mom?" Darcy said. "*My* pack is still inside."

"What?" her mother said, looking confused. "But I thought I got them all . . . wait a minute. Darcy, is *that* your bag?"

She was pointing at a giant red lump wedged against the window.

"Uh-huh," Darcy said guiltily.

"I thought it was an inflatable raft!" Victoria cried. "Did you pack your entire spring wardrobe for our little overnight?"

"No," Darcy said. "I packed only essentials. With a few tiny luxuries thrown in. And some emergency outfits. *And* maybe a couple spare ensembles."

"Darcy," Victoria said, planting her hands on her hips while a cluster of Jaybirds giggled nearby. "You know the rules. Each girl can bring only as much as she can carry. We still have to load up our tents and cooking supplies!"

"No worries!" Darcy said brightly. "I can totally carry this. See?"

Darcy reached into the van and slipped her slender arms through the pack's straps.

"See," she said as she heaved the pack out of the van. "No prob-LEM!"

Except, it sort of was. Because the minute Darcy hefted her backpack onto her shoulders, she fell right over! Now, still attached to the enormous pack, she was lying helplessly on her back like an upended turtle.

That did it. The Jaybirds' polite titters turned into loud, bellowing belly laughs!

"Start unloading, girlfriend," Lindsay laughed as she pulled Darcy to her feet.

"I have another idea," Darcy said, winking as she pulled out her cell phone. Sighing with relief to see that she had a glimmer of reception on her phone, she ducked to the other side of the van and made a speedy call.

What's that Jaybird motto? Darcy thought as she clicked her phone shut a moment later. *Be improvisational? Maybe I should be named an honorary bird after all!*

And why was that? Because a few minutes later, a battered pickup truck—dragging a trailer behind it—pulled up next to the Jaybirds' van. From the cab of the truck stepped two men in identical baseball caps and plaid shirts.

"Yay!" Darcy said, skipping up to the guys and giving them quick hugs. She turned to the Jaybirds, who were busy topping off their packs with tent poles, cooking supplies, and water bottles.

"Jaybird Scouts," Darcy announced. "I'd like to introduce our good friends, Brett and Brandon Brennan."

"We're the Brennan brothers," Brett said.

"Howdy," Brandon said.

"More importantly," Darcy added, "I'd like to introduce the *Brennans'* good friend, Oprah!"

Brett tromped to the back of the trailer and led out their doe-eyed, flappy-eared llama.

"As I'm sure you know," Darcy said proudly, "llamas are pack animals. They're excellent companions for a camping trip. And the Brennan brothers are very nicely letting us borrow Oprah for our trip. So all the extra stuff that we can't carry? Oprah can do the job!"

"Yay!" the Jaybirds cried, jumping up and down. Oprah, meanwhile, rolled her big brown eyes and flapped her lips at Brandon as if to say, *What have you gotten me into?*

Darcy held her breath until Brandon reached out and patted Oprah on her long, woolly neck.

"I know, honey," he said. "Jaybirds are loud. But they're also the source of mini muffins. And you know you love mini muffins!"

Oprah did a little tap dance on her soft two-toed feet, which Darcy took to mean *Will work for food!*

"Brett and Brandon!" Victoria trilled when she'd doled out the last of the supplies to the Jaybirds. "This is wonderful! What luck that Darcy could reach you!"

Victoria shot her daughter a sidelong glance, which made Darcy gulp.

"Oh, it was nothing," Brett said with a gap-toothed grin. "We were out in these parts anyway. We heard there was a one-eyed owl around here that keeps flying into trees, and we wanted to rescue it."

"And Oprah loves to travel, so we brought her along," Brandon said. "We were only a few miles away when Darcy called."

"Well, Darcy," Victoria said, giving her daughter a proud squeeze. "I was right about your leadership skills. That was a brilliant idea to call for aid."

"Thanks, Mom," Darcy said graciously.

"But," her mother added sweetly, "you still have to unload a good three-quarters of your backpack."

"Aw!"

"I'm sorry, dear," Victoria said. "Oprah can carry a few of our things, but now we'll also have to pack *her* supplies as well."

"Oh," Darcy said, kicking at the dirt with her sneaker toe. "I hadn't thought of that."

"Well, yeah," Brandon said. "Llamas can't live on mini muffins alone, you know."

He loped to the truck and pulled out a saddlebag.

"Now here's Oprah's feed and her multivitamins," he said, handing Darcy the heavy pack. "And her favorite toy for her afternoon playtime, her saddle blanket, and her sleeping mask."

"Sleeping mask?" Darcy squawked, pulling a black satin eye mask out of the bag.

"Oh yeah," Brett said. "Oprah can't sleep a wink when it's light-out."

"Oh-kay," Darcy said, shaking her head.

✳ DARCY'S TRAVEL JOURNAL ✳

Of all the llamas in the world, I get the one with a diva complex. They don't call her Oprah for nothing!

✳   ✳   ✳   ✳   ✳   ✳

So, Darcy's plan worked, sort of. The Jaybird
Scouts had a great time loading Oprah up with her
supplies as well as a few items that lightened their
own loads. And Darcy sighed her way through
unpacking her lip-gloss collection, all but one pair
of capris, every one of her strappy sandals, and even
her self-inflating, full-size air mattress. When she was
done, she'd whittled her pack down to little more than
a change of clothes and her toothbrush—just as her
mother had ordered.

But at least, Darcy consoled herself as the troop
set out for the hike to their campsite, *I retained one
element of luxury. My toothbrush? It's battery-operated!*

Chapter 10

Wild Wisdom . . . *Fox cubs are born blind and deaf. They develop sight and hearing soon after birth.*

As the troop tromped through the woods, Darcy breathed in deeply. Aside from the slight odor of Oprah, who was leading the way at a lazy lope, the air smelled sweet and green. The sun glimmered pleasantly through the treetops, dappling the Jaybirds' blue-beanied heads. And Victoria provided a running commentary, shouting out, "Look, girls! I think that's a spotted fox darting through the brush over there."

Or, "Behold this beautiful fern, Jaybirds. *Adantium pedatum,* I believe."

She even plucked a bit of gnarled fungus from the base of a tree and held it up to the group.

"This," she announced proudly, "is a morel mushroom. Highly gourmet and expensive in restaurants, but in the woods—it's free of charge. Anyone who spots a morel on our hike, pick it. At the end, perhaps we'll have enough for campfire-fried mushrooms. Delicious."

I gotta admit, Darcy thought as she hiked along, scanning the dirt for mushrooms, *I feel like my wilderness allergy is fading. I mean, this mushroom hunt? It's fun! So's all the girly companionship. And as for the trees, the sweet air, even this dirt path? They're totally pleasant. Who knew? I thought I would miss my iPod out here, but to tell the truth, I'm digging the sounds of the forest. The occasional bark of a fox or chirp of a bird. The breeze rustling the leaves. The—*

"Singing!"

Darcy jumped. Her mother had just moved onto a new activity for the girls' hike—and it filled Darcy with foreboding.

"Singing?" she said.

"Yes, we should be singing," Victoria proclaimed. "That's what one does on a hike. Remember *The Sound of Music*?"

"You want us to sing 'Climb Ev'ry Mountain'?!" Darcy squeaked. "Mom, Julie Andrews is so not hip. Are you sure the Jaybirds can relate?"

"Hmm, maybe you're right," Victoria said as the Jaybirds, Lindsay, and Kathi sighed with relief.

"I know!" Victoria said. "We'll do a round of 'White Coral Bells'! It's a lovely tune. Keri, Sophie, Lizzy, and Hannah, you take the first verse. . . ."

The Scouts looked at Darcy beseechingly.

"Sorry, dudes," Darcy whispered to them. "You know my mom when she sets her mind on something."

"Yeah," Lizzy whined. "I've still got the jam in my hair to prove it. I've become a blackberry blonde!"

Darcy giggled. "Just sing," she advised the little girl. "Before you know it, we'll make it to our campsite and have lunch. And I assure you, my mom isn't going to make us sing with our mouths full."

So the girls began warbling:

"*White Coral Bells,*

upon a slender stalk.

Lilies of the valley deck my garden walk. . . ."

And even that was fun—if totally goofy, unhip fun. Darcy couldn't help singing along to the sweet little tune.

The wilderness rocks! she thought happily.

Ugh, Darcy thought two miles later. *I just tripped over another rock. And that blister on my right heel? I think it must be about the size of a quarter by now.*

"*Oh, don't you wish,*" the Jaybirds sang,

"*That you could hear them ring.*

That will happen only when the fairies sing!"

Okay, and "White Coral Bells"? Darcy thought as she slapped away a mosquito. *I really could live without them ringing. Ditto for fairies singing. In fact, I think I need to take the matter of our musical accompaniment into my own hands!*

Just as the Jaybirds were about to launch into their forty-second round of "White Coral Bells," Darcy held up her hand.

"Um, excuse me?" Darcy called out. "Being new to the Jaybird ways and all, I need to know. What kind of system have we got going on here? A democracy? A theocracy? Dictatorship?"

"Why, Darcy," her mother said. "Of course we can vote on matters. What issue did you want to address?"

"I think we should take a vote on our musical choice," Darcy announced. She turned to the parade of Jaybirds. "All those in favor of continuing 'White Coral Bells,' raise their hands."

Victoria's lone hand rose into the air.

"All those who'd rather rock out to 'Miss Independent'?"

"Kelly Clarkson?" Sophie cried out. "Duh!"

Alissa and Lizzy immediately began harmonizing the song's intro while Hannah thumped out the drum rhythm on a tin cup. Then everybody began singing all at once.

To her mom's pained expression, Darcy called out, "Sorry, Mom! But the Jaybirds have spoken."

"No, we've sung!" Kathi said as she shimmied along to the tune. "Way to save the day, Darcy!"

Little does she know, Darcy thought with a sly grin, *Kelly Clarkson's not the only trick I've got up my sleeve! Have I got a surprise for them! But I can't pull it out until we've made it to our campsite!*

Which finally happened about an *hour* later. It had been a five-mile hike, but finally the Jaybird troop staggered into the clearing that was their campsite—a circle of logs surrounding a charred fire pit. Only a few feet away, through a thicket of lush trees, was a babbling river, and just up the stream was a waterfall! It was beautiful.

But everybody was too tired to appreciate it. All the hiking and singing, not to mention mosquito slapping and poison-oak dodging, had left them too exhausted to do anything except flop onto their log seats and huff and puff.

Only Ginny had the strength to form words.

"I'm *hungry!*" she said, clutching her stomach. "And we hardly found any morel mushrooms. What are we gonna eat?"

"Ginny," Darcy said with a proud smile, "say no more. I have a treat for you guys!"

"Really?!" said all the Jaybirds at once.

"Really?" Victoria echoed them.

Lindsay just raised one eyebrow and said, "Darcy,

I hope this isn't, like, pedicure supplies or something. We're supposed to be roughing it."

"Just because we're roughing it doesn't mean we can't eat well!" Darcy announced. "While you guys weren't looking, I was packing up Oprah's saddlebags with some gourmet treats! We're talking smoked salmon and brioche. An awesome field green salad. And for dessert, dried figs, honey, and gourmet chocolate!"

"Yay!!!" cried everyone in the group. Even Lindsay jumped up and down in hungry excitement.

"You rock," Kathi said. "I should have known that camping out with you and your mom would mean better grub than franks and beans and gorp and stuff."

"Gorp?" Darcy giggled. "What a weird word. What's that?"

"Oh, it's just a camping term for trail mix," Kathi said. "You know, nuts, raisins, chocolate chips, sunflower seeds, and stuff."

"Sounds yummy," Darcy said. "But Kathi, you're right. Gorp's not nearly as delicious as the feast I've got planned for us. Wanna help me unload Oprah?"

She pointed to the edge of the clearing, where the llama had plopped herself down for a post-hike lounge. As Darcy and Kathi headed over to her, Darcy grinned.

Oprah's so cute, she thought. *Look, she's nosing around in her saddlebag. And . . . she seems to be chewing on something! Wait a minute . . .*

"No!" Darcy breathed.

"What is it?" Kathi asked in alarm.

"Listen," Darcy whispered. Both girls cocked their heads toward Oprah.

Crunch, crunch, crunch.

"Nooooo!" Darcy cried. She pulled the saddlebag from Oprah's woolly back and peeked inside.

"Did she get the smoked salmon?" Kathi asked tremulously.

"Fished it right out of there," Darcy groaned as she rifled through the pack. "The brioche is gone, too! I think there may be a few figs left, but they're covered with llama spit!"

"Gross!" Kathi wailed.

Victoria trotted up behind her.

"Oh, what a shame," she cried, peeking into the packs over Darcy's shoulder. "Well, the good news is . . ."

Victoria dug into the bottom of the saddlebag and pulled out three shiny cans.

". . . Oprah left us all the franks and beans!" Victoria announced. "Now, Darcy, where did you pack that can opener?"

Darcy slapped her forehead and quoted her friend Eli, who was living in the lap of luxury back home.

"Aw, no!"

Chapter 11

Wild Wisdom . . . *Female prairie voles can give birth at just two months of age.*

"Aw, no!" Eli cried. He was sitting on the floor of the walk-in pantry, shaking a *mountain* of flour out of his hair.

Actually, a mountain of flour was an exaggeration. It would be more accurate to call the dusty white stuff on top of Eli's head a molehill. It would be even *more* accurate to call it a *vole hill*. Because, of course, the prairie voles were to blame!

Eli had been chasing the voles around the kitchen for the past twenty minutes. When he'd first stormed into the house, just after the voles had escaped their crate, he'd found the little critters cowering in the corner next to the dishwasher.

"Don't worry, little voles," Eli had crooned as he'd dropped to a crawl. "I'm not gonna hurt ya. C'mon! Come to Eli."

Eli reached out to the fuzzy brown critters with cupped hands. He smiled benignly. He moved carefully so as not to trip and startle the voles. Eli was always at his best around animals.

And it worked! He'd almost reached the little rodents!

Of course, that's when Eli's gentle attempt at entrapment went terribly wrong. When he was about a foot away from the voles, they let out a couple of shrill *bleets* and jumped backward—smacking square into the dishwasher door! While the voles scurried away, totally unharmed, the dishwasher swung open, clunking Eli right on the head.

"Whoa!" Eli moaned, slumping woozily to the floor. Luckily, Kevin had just arrived in the kitchen. He spotted the voles as they scratched their way into the cabinet that held the pots and pans.

Clang! Crash! Tinkle! Klung!

Eli and Kevin looked at each other from across the kitchen.

"Klung?" they said. Then they simultaneously dashed to the pot-and-pan cabinet.

"Okay, Dr. Adams," Eli whispered as the voles continued to bang around inside. "What's our plan?"

"Considering that these little rodents are likely to jump out of there any second now," Kevin said, "I say, improvise!"

"But I'm no good," Eli began, "at improv—"

Klunk!

Suddenly, the cabinet door sprang open and the voles hopped out!

"Improvise, improvise!" Kevin shrieked at his comrade.

In a panic, Eli grabbed a giant soup pot from inside the cabinet and tossed it Frisbee-style after the darting voles.

Of course, the pot missed the critters by a mile. It *did* manage to catch Kevin right in the kneecap.

"Ooh!" Kevin grunted, grabbing his leg.

"Aw, no!" Eli cried, slapping both hands to his head. "We need more manpower for this job. Can't Jack help?"

"Jack!" Kevin bellowed. "Where are you, son?"

Kevin and Eli both cocked an ear, but there was no response.

"We'll have to go on without him," Kevin panted, clutching his leg. "I just saw the voles head into the pantry. Go, Eli, go!"

Eli went. He dove into the pantry just as the voles ducked behind a row of cereal boxes. He pulled out the corn flakes. No voles. Behind the shredded wheat? A vole-free zone. The raisin bran and Darcy's cocoa pops were voleless, too! There was only one box of cereal left.

"Fat-free granola," Eli whispered. "Maybe the voles are on a diet!"

Holding his breath, Eli grabbed the cereal box and pulled it off the shelf. Cowering behind it were the prairie voles! Eli tried to grab them, but they slipped through his fingers—and ran right up the length of his arms! Plump Mrs. Vole scurried up Eli's left arm and wiry Mr. Vole scampered up the right. Together, the rodents leaped off Kevin's shoulders onto a high shelf, tipping over a big canister of flour as they went.

And *that* was how Eli came to be buried in that vole hill of whiteness. By the time he'd cleared the dust out of his eyes, the voles had disappeared entirely.

Of course, that's when Jack finally meandered into the kitchen. He blinked at his dad, who was still clutching his knee on the kitchen floor. Then he coolly regarded his flour-dusted friend, Eli.

"I thought I heard you guys calling me," he said. "But it looks like you've got things under control now."

"What?!" Eli squawked.

Jack clapped a hand on Eli's shoulder, unleashing a great cloud of flour.

"Eli, my friend," Jack rasped, shaking his head, "if you're ever going to make it out of Bailey, you're really gonna have to master the fine art of sarcasm."

"I don't want to leave Bailey," Eli moaned, hanging his head. "I just want to catch those voles."

"And how," Kevin said. "Now that they're good and spooked, I bet our voles are going to burrow as deep into the house as they can. It's going to be quite a trick tracking them down."

"Well! Good luck with that," Jack said, strolling past his dad to head for the back door. "If you need me, I'll be out back."

"Hosing yourself off, I hope?" Kevin said, pinching his nose. "Don't take any offense, son, but you smell like a garbage barge!"

Jack raised his eyebrows and lifted his arms to his face, giving himself a deep whiff. Then he flashed his dad a big smile.

"Yes, I do, Dad," he said. "Yes, I do!"

He sauntered out of the kitchen, cackling and rubbing his hands together while Kevin and Eli gaped after him.

"I don't know which is weirder, Dr. Adams," Eli said, "this prairie vole hunt or your son!"

Chapter 12

Wild Wisdom . . . *A grasshopper can hop up to twenty times the length of its body.*

"Ugh," Darcy said as she scooped her last gummy spoonful of franks and beans into her mouth. The troop was sitting in a circle around the campfire (expertly built by Ginny and April). "After this lunch, even Oprah's llama feed is looking attractive."

Lindsay shook her head.

"Darcy," she explained with an eye roll, "a camping trip is not about gourmet food. It's about being *away* from civilization. Come on, even *you* have to admit that all this woodsy air smells good. I think it makes the food taste better."

"Easy for you to say," Darcy countered. "You *already* like franks and beans."

Darcy twisted on the log she was sitting on and said to her mother, "We've got to come up with an alternative plan for dinner, Mom! I don't suppose pizza delivery is an option?"

"Not when a fabulous dinner is waiting for us just a few feet away!" Victoria protested.

All the girls perked up and began looking around.

"Where?" Ginny wondered. "Is there some kind of snack bar out here?"

"Dare I hope for a frozen yogurt hut?" Kathi said.

"I'd *kill* for a frozen yogurt," Keri cried.

"With Oreos and M&M's on top," Sophie added.

"Girls, girls!" Victoria admonished the Scouts. "Even if frozen yogurt *was* in the camping spirit, which it is *not . . .*"

The Jaybirds hung their heads in shame.

". . . we'd be out of luck," Victoria continued. "We are, after all, deep inside the Roaming Bear National Park."

"Which means we're much more likely to encounter a roaming bear," Lindsay pointed out with a devilish grin, "than a frozen yogurt stand."

"Thanks for the reminder, girlfriend," Darcy said drily. "Too bad we'll be too weak to run from that roaming bear on this diet of franks, beans, and no fro-yo."

"Who needs frozen yogurt," Victoria blurted in exasperation, "when you've got fish! A whole river of fish, right at our fingertips. My little Scouts, right after we pitch our tents, we're going to go wade for our supper!"

"Whoa," Hannah breathed with wide eyes. "Fishing for food is way advanced. In the Jaybird handbook, it's an activity reserved for teenage Scouts."

"Oh my," Victoria said, blanching. "I suppose I should have read the handbook with a bit more attention. But at five hundred and fifty pages, it's quite a job. Mrs. Toadst was a stickler for detail, wasn't she?"

"You get a badge for finishing it," Lizzy pointed out.

"Not surprising," Victoria said. "Well, girls, what do you think? Is fishing a bit much for your nine-year-old selves?"

"Wellll," a couple of the girls said nervously.

"Wait a minute, you guys," Lizzy jumped in, slamming her fist into her palm. "Don't wimp out. Here's what you would know if you *had* read the whole handbook. For catching fish, you get more than a badge. More than a medal, even! You get a rad, fish-shaped *trophy*!"

"Oooooh!"

Every Jaybird at the campsite began jumping in excitement. Even Oprah brayed with enthusiasm.

"Well, troop leader," Lizzy said, turning to Victoria

with a grin. "I think that's your answer. Let's get those tents up and go fishing!"

It turned out that tent pitching was another one of those outdoorsy feats that win Jaybird Scouts coveted badges. Which meant *all* of the seven scouts wanted a hand in the pitching of the group's supersized tent.

"I'll hammer the tarp to the ground!" Alissa announced.

"I'll stretch it out flat!" Lizzy added.

"I'll fit the stackable tent poles together," Hannah volunteered, pulling a bunch of skinny rods out of her backpack.

"And I'll unroll the tent top!" Keri cried.

"Oh no," Darcy said to Kathi and Lindsay with mock chagrin. "The Jaybird Scouts are so gung ho about this tent pitching, I don't think there's any room for us to help!"

"Horrors," Kathi joked. "Whatever shall we do?"

"I guess we have no choice but to flop down here and relax," Lindsay said, lounging on her log.

Darcy had just settled in next to her when her mother marched over with two tin cans. She thrust them into Darcy and Kathi's hands.

"Oh, is there a recycling bin you want us to put these in?" Darcy asked, smiling at her mom. "No prob,

Mom! We'll get on that right after we've had a little rest."

Victoria raised one eyebrow at her daughter.

DARCY'S TRAVEL JOURNAL

Anybody who's seen my mom's movies knows that the single raised eyebrow is her *trademark* move. The Fields Eyebrow is devastatingly withering. And when Mom broke it out just then, I knew I was in for it—and *it* was gross beyond words!

"Darcy," Victoria said. "That can is not for recycling—it's for collecting."

"Mushrooms?" Darcy said hopefully.

"Worms!" Victoria said. "As in fish bait. As soon as the girls are done pitching the tent, we've got to jump on our fishing expedition. Catching our dinner could take all afternoon."

"Ugh!" Darcy groaned while Lindsay started giggling.

"Oh, come on, Darce," Kathi said, giving Darcy a teasing poke in the arm. "Worms are harmless!"

"I'm glad you're so bug-friendly, Kathi," Victoria said, handing her the other can. "Because I'd like you to go find some grasshoppers and beetles and other insects.

Some fish are more attracted to creepy, crawly bugs, rather than slithery, slimy ones."

"Grubs!" Kathi shrieked.

By now, Lindsay was doubled over, she was laughing so hard. That is, until Victoria gave her *her* chore.

"And Lindsay," Darcy's mom added, "we're going to need a large assortment of firewood. Large logs, chunky sticks, and plenty of dried twigs for kindling. I trust you can handle that? You can take Oprah with you—she can carry the bigger branches in her saddlebags."

Lindsay swallowed her laughter.

"No problem, Mrs. Fields," she said. "Collecting firewood is totally necessary. And, might I add, bug-free!"

She cast another teasing glance at Kathi and Darcy.

Darcy rolled her eyes.

"I'd ask Lindsay to trade jobs," she whispered to Kathi, "but Mom wouldn't like it. Might as well get our bait hunt started."

"Ugh, guess you're right," Kathi sighed.

They headed into the woods.

Several screams and gasps later, they actually *had* collected a few beetles, grubs, and worms. They still had many more to gather, though, before they had enough for the whole troop to fish with.

"My dad always fishes with *artificial* lures," Kathi complained as she tromped deeper into the woods. "You know, little rubber bugs and floaties with feathers attached and stuff like that. *Real* bugs are hard-core!"

"Fake bugs," Darcy said, twirling one of the braids Sophie had made in her hair during lunch. "Now *there's* a concept."

The plastic beads on her braids' hair elastics clicked as she mused. Darcy glanced down at them. The beads were bright green and sparkly.

"Wait a minute," she suddenly exclaimed, "*here's* a concept! Kathi, I have an idea!"

Half an hour after Darcy had whispered her brainstorm into Kathi's ear, the Jaybirds gathered at the riverside, fishing poles at the ready.

"Now, everybody space yourselves out along the river's edge," Victoria said, hoisting her own pole, "and cast your hook gently, like so."

Victoria flicked her fishing pole. Its hook sailed into the air with a pleasant *zinnnggg* and plopped right into the middle of the water.

"But . . . how . . ." Darcy sputtered as Victoria reeled her hook back in. "Mom, I didn't know you knew how to fish!"

"Don't you remember my movie *Highwater Pants*?"

Victoria said. "I had to become an expert fly fisherwoman for that picture!"

"Oh yeah!" Darcy said. "You used to bring home all sorts of yummy fish from the set. Major inspiration! Let's fish, you guys!"

"Not without bait," Victoria said. "Let's see what you girls found."

The Jaybirds (plus Oprah, who'd come along to watch the girls in action) gathered around Darcy and peeked into her tin can.

"Hair elastics?" Sophie exclaimed, pulling out a handful of beaded rubber bands. She pointed at Kathi and Darcy's unbraided locks. "I put these in your hair!"

"And *now,* they're going to make perfect fishing lures," Darcy said. She plucked other bouncy beads out of the Jaybirds' braids.

"Artificial lures!" Darcy's mother said with a frown. "I'm not sure if that'll qualify the girls for their Jaybird fishing badges, Darcy."

"What?!" Keri cried. She turned to Darcy. "That reeks!"

"So does spearing a beetle on a fishhook," Darcy retorted. "But you're welcome to try it, if you want. Before I came up with the hair-elastic idea, Kathi did catch a couple of nice juicy ones."

"Uh-huh," Kathi said, holding up her can. She walked over to Keri.

"Here ya go," Kathi said as Keri backed away from her. "Just take one. But careful, they're crawly little suckers."

"Um . . . maybe hair beads *are* a good idea," Keri protested, backing up a few more steps. "Badges aren't everything."

"Are ya sure?" Kathi said, thrusting the can toward the little girl. "They're perfectly good beetles."

"O-okay," Keri quavered. "I guess it's the Jaybird thing to do. Hand one over."

She held out one hand reluctantly, and Kathi tipped the can carefully into it.

Not carefully enough, unfortunately! Instead of one beetle, about *ten* of them landed on Keri's palm.

Ten beetles amounts to sixty little legs.

Which is about fifty too many, even for a seasoned Jaybird Scout!

"Ahhh!" Keri cried. In full freak-out mode, she began flapping the beetles off her hand, screaming and jumping around all at once.

The good news was, she shook off all the beetles.

The bad news? With all that jumping, Keri accidentally jumped right into the river!

"Ack!" she sputtered, standing in the shallow water. She was soaked from sneakers to braids. Only the fluffy feather on top of her beanie was still dry.

But not for long, Darcy thought.

"Everybody who feels the same way about bugs as Keri does," Darcy announced, "grab your hair elastics and beanie feathers and start fishing with those!"

"Yay!" Keri cried, undoing her braids and plucking her beanie feather gleefully. The other girls gratefully did the same and began winding their sparkly hair beads into their fishhooks.

"Fried fish supper, here we come!" Darcy cried, flinging her bead-baited line into the river.

Or . . . maybe not.

Several hours later, Oprah had curled up for a riverside nap, and the Jaybirds didn't have *one* fish for their frying pan.

Oh, it wasn't the beads at fault. In fact, the shiny bait had lured fish after fish to the girls' hooks.

It was *keeping* the fish that was the problem.

Alissa was the first girl to snag a fish—a tiny, silvery thing that wiggled wildly in her hands. She looked at the fish in horror as it struggled for breath.

"I think that one's too small, Alissa dear," Victoria said after she'd taken a peek at Alissa's catch. "Good catch, but we should let it go and stick to more mature fish."

"Whew!" Alissa said gratefully as she plunked her

fish back into the water. "Swim away, Clyde. Be free!"

"Clyde!" Keri said. "You knew the fish for five seconds and you gave it a name?"

"He just . . . looked like a Clyde," Alissa shrugged. "I'm glad we don't have to eat him."

"Well what does *this* one look like?" Sophie yelled from her spot a few feet down the riverbank. Her troop members turned to see her proudly holding up a fat, wriggly trout.

"I just reeled it in," she announced.

"I know," Darcy said. "Let's call that one . . . Chloe!"

"A perfect match for Clyde," Kathi piped up.

"Unless, of course, *we eat her,*" Keri pointed out.

"We *can't* eat Chloe," Sophie cried, dropping her fish back in the lake. "In fact, I'm not sure if I can ever eat another fish again! They're too cute!"

"Aw!" Hannah said, staring at the fish *she'd* just caught. "You're right. Swim away, Susie!"

She plunked her fish back in the water, too.

"Chloe? Susie?" Lindsay sputtered from her spot on the riverbank. "What, are you all suddenly vegetarians? May I remind you that you're still digesting your *frank* and bean lunches?"

"I'm no vegetarian," Ginny protested. "But . . .

well, it's one thing to buy a McFishwich. It's another to stare your supper in the face before you eat it!"

"Yeah! Inhumane!" the Jaybirds chorused.

"Well, *I'm* not squeamish," Lindsay said, just as her fishing line started twitching in the river. "I'm hungry! And I intend to eat fish for dinner."

With a triumphant grunt, Lindsay pulled a fat fish out of the water and held it aloft proudly.

"Excellent, Lindsay," Victoria said. She handed Lindsay a curved knife and said, "Now all you have to do is clean it!"

"Right!" Lindsay said. She took the knife from Victoria and knelt to place her wiggly fish on the ground.

She raised her knife.

She poised it over the fish's white belly.

And then, she glanced up at her camping buddies. Half the Jaybirds' lips were trembling. The other half were looking a little green. Kathi's hands were slapped over her eyes, and Darcy's were clapped over her mouth.

Only Victoria was trying to look strong. And even with her Oscar-winning acting skills, it was a struggle.

"Geez, you guys!" Lindsay protested. "Do you *not* want to eat dinner tonight?"

"Of course we want dinner," Ginny said.

The other Jaybirds murmured in agreement.

"All right, then," Lindsay said. She frowned down at her fish and raised the knife again.

"Except—"

Lindsay dropped the knife on the ground and glanced up at Ginny with a weary sigh.

"Except what?" she said.

"Except," Ginny squeaked, "doesn't that fish look an awful lot like Clyde?"

❄ (DARCY'S TRAVEL JOURNAL) ❄

Any guesses as to what we had for dinner that night? I'll give you a hint. It so wasn't fish. I can't say I was sorry, either. Clyde and Chloe *were* totally cute.

And at least after our supper of *more* canned food, Mom consoled us with s'mores. A good thing, too. We needed to carbo-load. The next day, my mom informed us, we were going on a giant hike. Forget fireside ghost stories. *That* was all I needed to give me nightmares.

❄   ❄   ❄   ❄   ❄   ❄

Chapter 13

Wild Wisdom . . . *An anteater's tongue is about two feet long.*

"This is a nightmare!" Kevin exclaimed that night back at Victoria and Darcy's house.

"Well, it would be," Eli said gloomily, "if we could get any sleep. Those prairie voles are terrorizing us!"

The vet and the ranch hand were sprawled out on the couch in the living room. They could hear the prairie voles scrabbling behind the walls. The voles had trailed crumbs from the kitchen throughout the entire house. The walls were pockmarked with tiny holes made by the voles' claws. The legs of the kitchen table were nibbled, and the tub in Victoria's bathroom was dusted with vole hairs.

"I feel like we're trapped in a *Tom and Jerry* cartoon," Kevin groaned. "And we're Tom."

"Who?" Eli said wearily.

"You know, *Tom and Jerry,*" Kevin said. "The cartoon?"

Eli stared blankly at Kevin, who rolled his eyes and said, "Tom's this cat who is constantly chasing Jerry, this mouse. And Jerry outwits Tom at every turn, usually with something like a cast-iron skillet to the head, turning Tom's face into a skillet-size pancake. This would happen over and over and *over* again, but Tom *never* caught that mouse."

"Whoa," Eli said. "That's so depressing."

"I know," Kevin nodded.

"I mean, TV was pretty boring when you were a kid, huh?" Eli went on.

"What?" Kevin said. "Eli, I know I can beat around the bush sometimes, but you're *really* missing my point. . . ."

Kevin was just launching into one of his famous lectures, when Jack jogged into the living room holding a small silver camera.

"Hey, Dad," he interrupted breathlessly, "do you think Victoria would mind if I used her digital camera? It's for a project."

"A school project?" Kevin said, lifting his head wearily to regard his son.

"Oh, you know," Jack said vaguely.

Too tired to inquire further, Kevin nodded.

"I'm sure Victoria won't mind," he said, "as long as you're careful with it."

"No worries!" Jack said, running out of the room eagerly.

Kevin lifted his head again to peer after his son.

"Is it just me, or did Jack leave behind a distinctive odor?" he said. "Like coffee grounds and eggshells and old bananas?"

"And a hint of newsprint," Eli agreed. "With notes of dirt."

"I'm going to have to make sure he takes a bath later," Kevin sighed. "After we clean all the vole hairs out of the tub, of course. Eli, we've *got* to come up with a way to trap these invaders. We need a plan that's diabolically clever yet completely humane. Any ideas?"

"I guess luring them with food is out of the question," Eli sighed, glancing through the living-room door into the ransacked kitchen. "Not when the voles seem to have an all-access pass to the pantry!"

"And we can't use other prairie voles to attract our pair," Kevin said. "Prairie voles are faithful to a fault. They won't even look at another vole once they've formed a family unit."

"And they're definitely a family unit," Eli said with

a shudder. "Mrs. Vole is huge! Do you think she's gonna have her babies soon?"

Suddenly, Kevin hopped off the sofa.

"Eli, that's it! You're a genius."

"I am?" Eli said.

"Mrs. Vole is pregnant!" Kevin proclaimed. "That's her weakness. I remember when my wife was pregnant with Jack, she would have paid a thousand dollars for the perfect slice of apple pie. And oh, how many pillows did I have to buy before she had *just* the right one."

"Wow, getting ready to have a baby is hard work," Eli said.

"Why do you think Jack doesn't have a little brother?" Kevin said. "Anyway, I'm sure that's why the voles are tearing the house apart. Mrs. Vole is probably wildly uncomfortable, craving a different snack every few minutes and unable to decide on the perfect nest in which to give birth."

"Aw, man—a birth," Eli sighed. "That's always super-messy! And I've already got flour and sugar all over the place to clean up. Dr. Adams, we've *got* to get rid of these voles!"

"And now I know how!" Kevin said, cackling. He hustled toward the kitchen. "C'mon, Eli," he said. "We've got a lot of work to do."

Two hours later, Kevin and Eli were poised to pounce. Arrayed on the kitchen floor was everything a mom-to-be could wish for: a bowl of pickles and a bowl of ice cream, potato chips of every flavor, and half a dozen varieties of cookies. Since their pregnant prey was a prairie vole, the offerings also included some fragrant alfalfa sprouts, a pinecone smeared in peanut butter, a lovely field green salad, and a giant pile of sunflower seeds. They'd topped it all off by laying out bowls of water both plain and sugar-laced.

"And now," Kevin said, "the pièce de résistance. Nesting materials!"

He reached into a bag and pulled out a big swatch of velvet, followed by a chenille throw, a down-stuffed silk pillow, a cozy cotton quilt, and several different sizes of shoe boxes.

When he'd finished, he and Eli smugly shook each other's hands and sat down at the kitchen table.

"Now all we have to do is watch and wait!" Kevin said.

"With our crate!" Eli added, waggling his eyebrows and patting the vole crate, which was ready by his feet.

Eli and Kevin settled into their chairs. They waited. And watched. And waited some more. When after half an hour, Eli yawned loudly and shifted in his chair, Kevin said, "Don't get discouraged, son. They're just teasing us. They'll be here any minute now."

After fifteen more minutes, Eli sighed and said, "Definitely within the next hour, right?"

"Defiiiinitelyyyy," Kevin said through a yawn of his own.

Two hours later, Jack bounded into the kitchen.

"Dad!" he yelled.

"Mhuh?!"

Kevin was so startled, he fell out of his kitchen chair. Maybe that was because he'd been *sleeping* in his kitchen chair.

Eli, meanwhile, was stretched out across two chairs, snoring loudly.

Blearily, Kevin glanced at his elaborate pregnant-vole trap. The peanut-buttered pinecone had disappeared, along with the pickles! And the medium-size shoe box and the silk pillow were gone!

"No!" Kevin shouted. Eli awakened with a snort and fell to the floor.

"We blew it, Eli," the vet sighed. "The voles came—and went—while we were sleeping."

"Aw, no!" Eli moaned.

Jack, meanwhile, was rolling his eyes.

"Y'know, when it comes to hobbies, vole trapping

doesn't look very fun," he said. "You should try something else."

"Thanks for the tip, Jack," Kevin said wearily. "Hey, have you had dinner? How about a field-green salad with some . . . erm, sour cream and onion potato chips on the side?"

"I can't eat, I'm too excited," Jack said, bouncing in place.

"Well *I* can't eat because you smell like trash, Jack!" Eli complained, waving a hand in front of his nose.

"Eating, bathing, that's all gotta wait," Jack said, brushing Eli off. "And for that matter, so does any Internet use. I'm gonna be on Victoria's computer for a while, okay?"

"Doing what, Jack?" Kevin asked, raising his eyebrows.

"Well, you know how I was using the digital camera," Jack said. "I'm uploading the pictures onto the Web now so I can . . . make a movie! With this . . . online editing program."

"And only a few digital pictures?" Eli said.

"It's more of a slide show, really," Jack said, his eyes darting back and forth excitedly. "It's the latest thing in Hollywood, haven't you heard? It's very indie, very Sundance."

"Well, Jack," Kevin said, putting a hand on his son's stinky head. "I really admire your ambition. You'll be the toast of L.A. someday. But if you're going to be a hit at those Hollywood power lunches, you *do* know that you'll have to take the occasional bath, right?"

"Dad," Jack said, slapping a hand onto his father's arm (and leaving a greasy smudge on his sleeve while he was at it), "I'm glad we had this little chat. If you need me, I'll be in the home office."

"Dr. Adams," Eli said, shaking his head as Jack trotted out of the kitchen, "I've said it before, and I'll say it again . . ."

"I know, I know," Kevin said wearily. "My son is acting weird. And our prairie voles are still at large. Boy, I envy that Jaybird troop right now. While we're here in crisis mode, they're having the time of their lives out in the woods!"

Chapter 14

Wild Wisdom . . . *The yellow-bellied sapsucker is a species of woodpecker. Twenty percent of its diet is made up of sap—talk about a sugar buzz!*

"Ahhhhhh! Help! Help meeeeee! Somebody help me—I'm lost in the woods!"

Darcy bolted upright in her sleeping bag. It was pitch-black, so Darcy groped for her flashlight. Flicking it on, she scanned the terrified faces of the Jaybirds—until she spotted an empty sleeping bag with a half-eaten s'more near the pillow.

"It's Ginny!" Darcy cried, jumping to her feet. Lindsay and Victoria kicked themselves out of their sleeping bags, too.

"Kathi, you stay with the other Jaybirds," Victoria said urgently. "Don't worry, girls, we'll be right back!"

Plunging out of the tent (well, after they'd tripped over at least three sleeping-bagged Jaybirds), Darcy, her mom, and Lindsay shone their flashlights into the trees.

"Ginny?" Darcy screeched. "Where are you?"

"I don't know," Ginny's voice squeaked from somewhere near the river. "My flashlight burned out, and I got all turned around."

"Well, just keep making noise, and we'll find our way to you," Lindsay ordered her. "Don't move, Ginny!"

Ginny responded with complete silence.

"Um, Ginny?" Darcy screamed. "Are you okay?"

"You said not to move," Ginny screeched back. "So I froze."

"*Don't* move your feet," Darcy said. "*Do* move your mouth. Just keep talking."

"Well, what should I say?" Ginny whined. "Please don't make me sing 'White Coral Bells' again. I don't think I can stand it."

"I know!" Victoria said. "Do the Jaybird call, Ginny! Just keep on cooing and cawing, and we'll get to you."

"Okay!"

Ginny launched into a string of *Coo-coo-coo-Caw-caw-caw-Kachings*!

"I never thought I'd say this, but that's music to my ears," Darcy said to Lindsay as they picked their way through the brush toward Ginny's voice. In a moment, Victoria and the girls had tracked the scared

Jaybird down in a thicket of trees. When they shined their flashlights on her, she was shivering in her night-gown.

"What are you doing out here!" Victoria cried, rushing over to give Ginny a hug.

"I ate too many s'mores and had a stomachache," Ginny said, clutching her middle. "I thought taking a little walk would help. But then my flashlight went kaput, and I couldn't find my way back!"

"Well, you shouldn't have gone in the first place," Victoria said sternly. "Not without me or one of the older girls."

"Sorrrryyyy," Ginny said, hanging her head in shame.

"It's okay," Victoria said, giving her a squeeze. "Just don't do it again, missy!"

"And good job on those Jaybird calls," Darcy added encouragingly.

"Let's get back to sleep," Lindsay sighed, leading the way back to the tent. As they picked their way through the woods, Darcy felt her mom's hand on her shoulder. It clamped down heavily, and to tell the truth, it was kind of clammy! It was stinky, too!

"Uh, Mom?" Darcy said. "I know that was scary and all, losing Ginny, but *I'm* fine. You don't have to hang on to my shoulder like that."

"What was that, darling?" Victoria said—*from several feet ahead of Darcy*!

Skidding to a halt, Darcy aimed her flashlight beam behind her.

What Darcy had thought was her mother's hand was the clammy, stinky chin of a llama!

"Ahhh!" Darcy screamed.

Unfazed, Oprah reached out with her long, slobbery tongue and gave Darcy's face a big lick.

"Ewwww!" Darcy shrieked, jumping about three feet into the air. Startled, the llama gave a jump herself. Then she started *spitting,* spraying Darcy with llama drool.

"Double ew!" Darcy screeched. Oprah merely sniffed and trotted back to the campsite, while Lindsay, Victoria, *and* Ginny burst out laughing.

"Glad I could break the tension," Darcy grumbled, scrubbing at her drooly cheek. "I just hope I can get back to sleep after all the *kachinging* and licking and stuff."

"Don't worry, Darcy," Victoria said, wiping the laughter tears from her eyes. "For your troubles, you get to sleep in tomorrow."

"Up and at 'em!" Victoria's voice trilled into the misty morning air. Darcy—along with every other girl in the tent—groaned and opened one eye to glance at her watch. Then she gasped and sat up to stare at her mother. Victoria was outside, peeking through the transparent mesh tent wall. Next to her, Oprah was chewing her cud and smugly blinking her long lashes at the sleepy girls.

"What?" Darcy squeaked. "It's six-thirty, Mom! I thought you said we could sleep in!"

"And you did," Victoria said. "I was *going* to get you girls up at six! Now hup, hup, my birdies. I've already got the kettle on for breakfast."

"Ooh, what are we having?" Darcy said hopefully. "Hot chocolate? Poached eggs?"

"Instant oatmeal!" Victoria announced, to more general groanage. "Why the complaining?" Victoria scolded. "Oatmeal is nutritious and filling, which is good. We've got ten miles to hike today, girls."

Oprah flapped her lips happily. Ten miles was nothing to her strong llama legs.

"Ten miles!" Darcy blurted as she crawled out of the tent. "This overnight is beginning to feel like blue-beanie boot camp!"

But of course, once the girls had rubbed the sleep from their eyes, slurped down their bland oatmeal, and set out for their day hike, things started to look up.

Literally.

"Girls," Victoria announced as they began their tromp, "I have good news and good news. The good news is, we're on our way to one of the most gorgeous views in the tristate area. It's really, really stunning."

"And the other good news?" Kathi asked eagerly.

"To get there," Victoria announced, "we've got to climb a rock."

She pulled from her daypack a tangle of rope and harnesses and pointed at a mountainous chunk of granite directly in the girls' path.

"A really, really big rock!"

"Helllllllppp!" Hannah cried as she swung in midair from her tether rope. She flailed her arms and legs and squealed like a baby bird knocked from its nest.

Down on the ground, Darcy and Kathi held on to Hannah's rope and gently lowered her to the ground.

"Okay, Mom?" Darcy said, wiping her brow. "That's the fifth Jaybird we've rescued from the really big rock. This climbing expedition is a wash!"

"But how will we get on with the rest of our hike if we don't scale the rock?" Victoria said, biting her lip. She glanced at her trail map. "I can't believe we're failing from the first step!"

"I'm sorrrry!" Hannah wailed. She looked at her

large digital watch and then at the detailed agenda she'd written on her clipboard. "We're way behind schedule, and it's all my fault."

"Don't blame yourself!" Darcy insisted as she helped Hannah take off her rock-climbing helmet. "Blame the really, really big rock."

Darcy looked up at the rock and scowled.

Thhhpppfffftt!

Darcy jumped and looked around.

"Um, don't look now," she said, "but I think the rock just gave me a razzberry!"

As the rest of the troop gasped and looked up at the rock, a familiar, floppy-eared face peeked over the top of it.

"Oprah!" the Jaybirds squealed.

Thhhpppfffftt!

"How did she get up there?" Darcy cried.

That's when Ginny put her wandering to good use—and spotted a path at the base of the rock. It turned out that the trail squiggled its way up the hill and, in a more roundabout way, landed at the rock's top! Within minutes, the Jaybirds had joined Oprah, who was taking in the beautiful view.

"All in favor of rewarding our llama with a few Jaybird mini muffins?" Darcy called out.

"Aye!" the group cried en masse.

Once they were all atop the rock, Victoria decided that their elevated perch was perfect for bird-watching.

"Hey," Keri suggested, "why don't we use our Jaybird call to attract the birds to us!"

"Um," Darcy quavered, "are you sure about tha—"

"Everyone got their binoculars?" Keri interrupted her.

"Check!" the other Jaybirds replied.

"Cameras?"

"Check!"

With that, the seven Jaybird Scouts unleashed an earsplitting *Coo-coo-coo-Caw-caw-caw-Kaching!*

"SQUAWK!" Flap, flap, flap.

"Look!" Darcy cried, pointing skyward as a great rustling filled the air. The Jaybird call had worked! Dozens of birds had left their hiding places in the trees and taken flight.

"There they are!" Victoria cried. "What do you see, girls? Any pileated woodpeckers? Yellow-bellied sapsuckers? Tufted titmice?"

"All I see are a bunch of bird *tails*!" Sophie blurted. "Flying *away*!"

"I guess," Darcy said, stifling a giggle, "the Jaybird call was a little *too* effective."

✳ ⟨ DARCY'S TRAVEL JOURNAL ⟩ ✳

I cannot tell a lie. We were getting discouraged. The rock climbing and bird-watching had been a total bust. And as for the next item on our agenda—lunch? I was sighing big and mighty sighs as I pulled out the can opener.

✳ ✳ ✳ ✳ ✳ ✳

"Here ya go, Mom," Darcy said as she handed the dreaded device to her mom. "What's it gonna be this time? SpaghettiOs? Spam? Or some other canned delight I haven't heard of?"

"Oh, I'm sorry, darling," Victoria said, biting her lip. "It looks like I'm going to disappoint you again."

Darcy sighed.

"Because," Victoria continued, unzipping her day pack, "I don't have *any* cans in here. Only some home-made scones and English sausages that I brought as a little surprise. Would you prefer Spam?"

"Mom, you're the best!" Darcy cried, throwing her arms around Victoria.

"Please," her mom muttered. "If I had to eat one more tinny meal, I was going to scream."

"Just as long as you don't do a Jaybird call," Darcy joked.

Chapter 15

Wild Wisdom . . . *Eastern bluebirds live in tree holes, which are usually excavated by woodpeckers.*

The troop ate their feast on a peak overlooking miles of beautiful woodlands.

"Now *this* is the life!" Darcy said as she popped her last bite of sausage into her mouth. She stretched out on the grass and laid her head on her daypack. "I could lounge here all afternoon, soaking in the rays and smelling the flowers."

"Um, Darcy," Lizzy said as she braided Kathi's hair nearby, "you're not so familiar with the Jaybird Scout handbook, so lemme fill you in on a little something."

"Yeah?" Darcy said, opening one eye to glance at Sophie.

"You don't get *badges* for just sittin' around all day!" Lizzy yelled.

"Duh!" Sophie seconded. "I'm craving a challenge. Troop leader, what've ya got?"

"I'm glad you asked, Sophie," Victoria said, dabbing her lips with a napkin and getting to her feet. "Ladies, I propose . . . a contest!"

"Like *Survivor*?" April piped up.

"Or *Fear Factor*?" Keri said.

"Can I just state for the record that I *refuse* to eat bugs?" Alissa said. "Badge or no badge. They're not kosher."

"Oh my word," Victoria blurted. "You girls really must get out more. In fact, that is the point of our contest, my little birds. I am challenging you to open your eyes and ears, to listen to your senses and discover nature!"

Victoria made her speech with starry eyes and grand flourishes, until Keri butted in with her usual bluntness.

"Uh, what're we talking about here?" she said. "Last I checked, there were no watching or listening badges."

Victoria thrust a sheet of paper into Keri's hands.

"I want you to start tracking all varieties of flora and fauna," she said. "You'll divide into teams and head down this trail."

Victoria pointed at a nearby tree painted with a red slash. The trail was marked every few feet with these slashes.

"Every animal, plant, fungus, or tree that you see—and can name—shall be recorded on your team's sheet of paper," Victoria announced. "And at the end, the winning team will be awarded with . . . the Toadst Medal."

"Oooohhhh," the Jaybirds (and Kathi) breathed.

"The toast medal?" Darcy shrugged. "I don't get it!"

"Toadst!" Kathi corrected her.

"Oh, right, the founder lady," Darcy said. "Well, what's so special about this medal?"

"It's dipped in 18-karat gold, for one thing," Hannah noted.

"Wow," Darcy said, lifting her eyebrows. "Those mini muffins *are* profitable."

"For another, all holders of the Toadst Medal get a free ticket to SplishSplash Water Park," Lizzy said. "And girls? Mark my words. By the end of the day, I'll be puttin' on my bathing suit!"

"Oh yeah?" Sophie challenged her.

"Yeah!" Lizzy said.

"I'll take a piece of that action," Keri cried, jumping to her feet. "Let's go!"

Within minutes, the girls had been divided into three teams led by Victoria (along with Oprah), Lindsay together with Kathi, and Darcy. Darcy was

totally psyched about her brood: Ginny, Alissa, and
Sophie.

*Ginny's so quiet and thoughtful, she'll totally spot
stuff the rest of us might miss,* Darcy thought. *And
Sophie's kind of a know-it-all, so she'll be able to identify
lots of stuff. And Alissa? Well, she's really tall! So she'll
be able to see things at her eye level that the other girls
might not.*

*The only weak link is . . . um, I guess me. Let's face
it. I'm a fabulous companion on a hike through a mall.
I can spot a Tuleh skirt on sale from a mile away. But
out here in the wilderness? I can barely tell the difference
between a morel mushroom and a mockingbird. Until a
couple days ago, I'd never even heard of the Toast medal!
I mean, Toadst.*

*What if I drag the girls down? What if it's me who
stands between them and their badges?*

Darcy hung her head, feeling majorly bummed
until she felt a tug at her long hair. She peeked over
her shoulder to see Sophie weaving her blond strands
into a pretty braid.

"I'm glad you're leading our team," Sophie said,
glancing up shyly from the braid in Darcy's hair.

"Really?" Darcy said incredulously.

"Duh!" Sophie said. "You're really fun. And even
though you're older than we are, you don't pretend to

know everything about everything. You kinda treat us as equals."

"Sophie, that's so sweet!" Darcy said, grinning at the young girl as she snapped an elastic around the base of her braid. "I just hope I can live up to your confidence in me."

"Me too!" Sophie said, jumping to her feet. "If I don't get that Toadst Medal, I'll just *die*."

"No pressure or anything," Darcy muttered as she got to her feet and followed Sophie over to Ginny and Alissa. Everybody was chattering excitedly until Victoria raised her hand.

"All right," she said. "The groups will head down the trail at five-minute intervals. The trail forms a five-mile loop so everybody will end up right here where we started. Whatever you do, leaders, make sure you stick to the trail with the red slashes. As long as you do, it will be impossible to get lost."

Easy enough, Darcy told herself nervously. *Just stick to the red slashes and try to avoid giving Sophie the biggest disappointment of her life!*

Darcy nibbled her fingernail anxiously as Kathi and Lindsay's group headed into the woods. When five minutes had passed, Victoria motioned Darcy and her Jaybirds onto the trail.

"Here we go," Darcy said, slinging her arms

around Ginny and Alissa's shoulders. "This'll be fun, huh?"

"Fun is not the point!" Sophie said as she darted ahead of them. "Winning is."

"Whatev," Alissa said, rolling her eyes. In mid eye roll, however, she froze. And pointed upward.

"Hey, I know what that tree is," she exclaimed. "It's a chestnut oak. My grandparents have a bunch of them on their farm."

"Excellent!" Darcy cried, digging her sheet of paper out of her pants pocket.

No sooner had she written the tree ID down than Sophie coolly announced, "Lizard! It's a six-lined race-runner!"

"Oooh," Darcy said as she watched the tiny critter scamper up the trunk of the chestnut oak. "So cute!"

A moment later, Ginny had rattled off the names of three ground-hugging ivies, Alissa had spotted a school of tadpoles in a thin stream that ran alongside the path, and Sophie had plucked a couple of mushrooms from the base of a tree.

"More morels!" she crowed, before holding the mushrooms to the top of her head. "Don't they look like horns? Look at me—I'm an alien!"

"You're a regular E.T.," Darcy giggled. "Wasn't he really into plants?"

"Like . . . these ox-eyed daisies!" Ginny cried,

pointing to a big cluster of little white blooms. She'd been munching on some trail mix as she searched, but she stopped snacking for a moment to pluck a few of the wildflowers. She quickly wove them into a daisy chain and plunked the petally crown onto Darcy's head.

"Queen Darcy," she dubbed her with a giggle. Darcy laughed, too, as her Jaybirds began scurrying around, identifying several more plants, bugs, and birds.

Darcy was having a fabulous time, and from the sounds of the other Jaybirds, whose voices were echoing through the woods, so were the other teams.

Darcy's only regret was that *she* hadn't identified a single thing.

I'm not much help at all, am I? she thought, looking around with a sigh. And *that's* when she spotted something, about fifty feet off the trail. It was a beautiful yellow flower, almost buried beneath a bunch of frothy ferns.

Hey, wait a minute, she told herself. *I may not know what that flower is, but I know it's something special. And it's so hidden, maybe the other groups haven't spotted it!*

Darcy stepped off the trail. "Hey, guys," she called to Sophie, Ginny, and Alissa, "check this out."

Together, they tromped through the brush to Darcy's yellow flower.

"Oooh, that's a celandine poppy," Alissa breathed.

"That's a good one!"

"Ooh, and look over there," Sophie yelled. "There's some butterfly milkweed."

"Sweet!" Ginny said, darting farther into the woods. Darcy followed, scribbling away at her lengthening list of flora and fauna.

This is way cool, Darcy kvelled. *Watching these girls totally master this contest is almost as fun as doing it myself!*

It was only after Darcy's team had pounced on three more natural wonders (an Eastern bluebird, some funky green lichen creeping up a tree trunk, and some purple buffalo clover) that Darcy noticed something else.

Or rather . . . the *absence* of something.

The voices of the other Jaybirds and leaders that had been echoing through the woods? And Oprah's lip-flapping brays? They'd disappeared! When Sophie, Ginny, and Alissa's chatter paused, Darcy heard nothing but a chilling silence.

Feeling her stomach swoop, Darcy whirled around to orient herself.

Except . . . she couldn't! The trail they'd strayed from seemed to have disappeared! And when Darcy looked desperately from tree to tree, she didn't see one red slash.

Oh, no! Darcy thought, covering her mouth with her hand. *I've gotten us lost!*

Chapter 16

Wild Wisdom . . . *Tufted titmice are very noisy, very social birds. They will come to the sound of human voices and even eat from our hands.*

Darcy was wringing her hands and trying not to hyperventilate.

The girls are gonna freak when they realize we're lost, she thought. *Unless . . . I don't tell them! I mean, isn't it my job as the team leader to protect my Jaybirds from unnecessary angst? I got us into this, I should get us out. But how . . .*

Darcy studied the girls as they searched for more species. Sophie was zigging and zagging all over the place, which made Darcy groan quietly.

If we've been following Sophie's path, who knows which direction we came from?

Then Darcy glanced at Ginny. As she picked her way through the forest plants, Ginny had been steadily dipping into her plastic bag of seeds, nuts, and dried fruit. But she was so preoccupied with the nature hunt that she was dropping as many bits of gorp as she ate.

And if I know Ginny, Darcy told herself hopefully, *she's been nibbling like this during our entire search!*

"Hey, guys!" Darcy called out, clenching her hands into fists so the girls wouldn't see them trembling. "I know something fun we can do. Let's pretend we're trackers. Ginny's been dropping gorp like a modern-day Gretel over there. Let's follow her gorp trail and see what we find?"

"But if Ginny made that trail," Sophie pointed out, "then she already covered that ground. We should move onward instead."

Leave it to Sophie to have an answer for everything, Darcy thought desperately. *So what's* my *answer going to be?*

She took a deep breath and threw out the first thing that popped into her head (no matter how ridiculous it was).

"Don't you know . . . about the law of second looks?" Darcy said.

"The what?" Sophie said impatiently.

"It's totally a law of physics," Darcy improvised. "Which you would know if you were in high school, like me. To put it simply, the law of second looks means that you'll see twice as much on your second look at something as you do on the first."

"Really?" Alissa said skeptically. "I've never heard of that."

"Wait until you take high-school physics," Darcy said with a vigorous nod. "It's one of the first things you'll learn. But why wait until high school? You'll learn it now when you follow Ginny's gorp trail."

"Okay," Sophie said reluctantly. "I just hope your physics teacher knows what she's talking about, or we could be chasing a trail toward third place."

Darcy pointed at a couple of peanuts on the ground.

"Ah-ha," she said, way too brightly. "The beginning of the trail."

"Hey!" Ginny said, running a few steps back and laughing. "Here's a chocolate chip! And right next to it is some rock cap moss that I didn't notice before!"

She turned to gaze at Darcy excitedly.

"You were so right with that physics thing," she said. "Man, it's cool being a teenager!"

Oh yeah, being in charge of three kids and endangering them by getting them lost in the woods? Darcy thought grimly. *Really cool.*

Luckily, the Jaybirds were oblivious to her angst. They were too excited about following Ginny's trail of dropped snacks. Exclaiming over each discovered nut, raisin, or sunflower seed, they quickly made their way back through the woods.

And back toward the trail, Darcy thought hopefully. *Can it be that my little Hansel and Gretel idea is actually working?*

Uh, that would be no. An instant after the thought flickered through Darcy's mind, the three Jaybirds let out a collective groan.

"Oh, no," Sophie said. "Look!"

Rushing up, Darcy peeked over the girls' shoulders to see—a fuzzy brown rabbit, busily munching on a peanut.

It was one of Ginny's peanuts!

"The bunny ate our trail!" Sophie complained.

"On the plus side, we don't have a rabbit on our list," Alissa pointed out. "And this guy is clearly of the genus Oryctolagus cuniculus."

Darcy didn't have time to be wowed by Alissa's rabbit identification. With their gorp gone cold, she had to figure out another way to find their way back to their Jaybird troop. Putting a hand to her forehead, she whirled around, looking again for signs of the trail.

And suddenly, she spotted one on a tree about a hundred feet away.

"A red slash!" she breathed. "Thank goodness!"

Darcy sprinted toward the marked tree, breath-less with relief until—the red slash suddenly flew away! Because it wasn't a paint slash at all! It was just a flame-red cardinal that had perched on the tree's branch for a moment.

When Darcy looked wildly at every other tree in the area, she saw that they were slashless, too!

Deflated, she turned back to the Jaybirds. They were staring at her with wide eyes and open mouths.

Whoops, Darcy thought with a sigh. *Not only did I spot a phantom red slash—I also blew my cover!*

Sophie, Ginny, and Alissa were looking from tree to tree themselves now. They were also craning their necks to spot the trail. When they didn't see any of the above, they returned their gaze to Darcy, their eyes filled with fear.

"That wasn't a game, finding the gorp trail!" Ginny cried.

"And it had nothing to do with physics," Sophie said. "It was about us being *lost*!"

Chapter 17

Wild Wisdom . . . *Aardvarks eat termites—and they've done so for the past 35 million years. They trap the insects inside their long, sticky tongues.*

Meanwhile, back at *Château Vole*, er, that is, *Château Fields*, Kevin and Eli had reached the ends of their ropes, too. They were flopped down at the kitchen table, their heads in their hands. The only sound in the house was the scrabbling of the two prairie voles somewhere out of sight—and the sound of Jack in Victoria's office, clicking madly on the computer.

"Dr. Adams," Eli said wearily, "we've tried everything. Pouncing. Trapping. Luring Mrs. Vole with pickles and ice cream."

"And don't forget playing the *Baby Story* marathon on the Ladies Network," Kevin said, pointing to the still-flickering TV in the living room.

"Ugh, don't remind me," Eli groaned. "I had to watch a dozen women giving birth on all those *Baby Story* shows. Talk about gross!"

"Eli," Kevin admonished him, "the miracle of birth is a beautiful thing."

"I'm not talking about the births," Eli said. "I'm talking about the commercials in between—all those weird cellulite creams and blackhead-removing strips and fat-free, sugar-free snacks. Yich!"

"Oh yeah, I'm with you there," Kevin said wearily. "You know, Eli, it's hard to be a woman. Especially a pregnant one."

"Well, from the sound of those guys, it's even harder being a pregnant vole!" Eli complained.

Kevin cocked his head. Eli was right. The prairie voles' *bleats* and *squawks* had indeed taken on a different tone. They were more urgent and agitated than ever.

"Maybe Mrs. Vole ran out of pickles and pinecones and she's desperate for a snack," Kevin said. "Believe me, those cravings can be powerful."

"Uh . . . Dr. Adams?" Eli quavered.

"Why, I remember when we were expecting Lindsay," Kevin reminisced, "my wife woke me up at three in the morning. 'A cheesesteak sandwich,' she told me. 'I must have one. NOW!' "

"Dr. Adams!" Eli squeaked.

"And then there was the watermelon-sorbet craving," Kevin laughed. "I mean, it was the dead of winter. My wife was eight and a half months pregnant with Jack, and all she wanted was watermelon sorbet. Homemade! That was a challenge, I tell ya!"

"Dr. Adams!" Eli shrieked. "We've got another challenge coming right at us. Look!"

Eli finally managed to jolt Kevin out of his flash-back—in time to see the male prairie vole scampering across the kitchen floor and heading straight for them!

"Grab the crate!" Eli shrieked. "Grab a cardboard box! Grab *anything*."

"Wait," Kevin said, holding up his finger. "This is highly unusual, this wild creature approaching us. Let's see what Mr. Vole has to say."

"Ex-*cuse* me?" Eli said. "We've lost the last twenty-four hours of our lives to this little dude, and you want to just have a chat with him?"

Kevin didn't take his eyes off Mr. Vole.

"Call it father's intuition," Kevin said. "Or vet's intuition, if you prefer. Maybe paternal veterinary sixth sense?"

"I get the idea," Eli grumbled. "Okay, you're the boss. I'm just saying that we might be missing our one and only chance to snag these little buggers."

"Or our chance to help them," Kevin said.

By the time he'd finished his sentence, the prairie vole had arrived at the vet's feet. It looked up at him and *bleated* wildly. The vole nosed at the toe of Kevin's shoe and began to run toward the front hall.

"See?!" Eli shrieked. "He's getting away!"

At that, the vole turned around and ran *back* to Kevin's shoe. Again, he tapped Kevin's toes with his nose, then took off toward the hallway. Kevin sprang to his feet and began following Mr. Vole.

"He's not getting away," he announced to Eli. "He wants us to come with him!"

"What?" Eli cried. He followed Kevin to the front-hall closet. Mr. Vole scratched at the closet door and it creaked open.

"Man," Eli scowled, "while we were *not* catching them, these voles really learned the lay of the land."

"Yup!" Kevin said proudly. "And that's how Mrs. Vole chose the perfect place to have her babies."

He pointed to the floor of the hall closet, where Mrs. Vole had made a cozy circle of Darcy's sneakers and Victoria's garden clogs. Inside that circle was the shoebox she'd stolen, lined with the down from the silk pillow.

"Smart vole," Kevin said. "It's warm and dry in here, and since it's not winter, this coat closet is barely being used right now. Our vole couple can burrow in here, give birth, and nurse their young through their first days of life."

"Give . . . birth?" Eli said, going pale. "Y'mean . . . now?!"

"Looks that way," Kevin said. "What's the big deal, Eli? You just saw a dozen people give birth on those *Baby Story* shows. And surely, you've seen lots of barnyard animals have babies. You know it's no big deal."

"Yeah, but this is different," Eli said. "These are wild animals. Wild animals who've been *terrorizing* us. Who knows what they're capable of when there are labor pains involved. I don't know if I can hack it, Dr. Adams."

"You don't have to, Eli," Kevin said patiently. "I'm a vet, remember?"

"Oh . . . oh yeah!" Eli said, brightening. "Hey, that must be why Mr. Vole came to you for help."

"Yeah, he's freaking," Kevin said, gazing affectionately at Mr. Vole. The little guy was hovering by the toe of Kevin's shoe, wringing his front paws and looking bugeyed and twitchy. "No matter how prepared dads are, when the babies actually get ready to arrive, they always freak."

Kevin reached down and stroked the vole's head with his fingers. "Don't worry, little vole," he said. "I'm here to help."

And help he did. Within a couple of hours, Mrs. Vole had safely delivered *six* squirming babies. Mr.

Vole's panic had died down and the entire prairie vole family had fallen asleep in their makeshift nest.

"Mr. Vole even licked my hand," Kevin announced to Eli after he'd rejoined him in the living room. (Eli had spent the labor and delivery watching TV. In fact, he'd watched a *Baby Story*. He'd sort of gotten hooked during the long vole stakeout.)

"I was absolutely right," Kevin said with a happy sigh, "when I said that Mr. Vole would calm down after the babies arrived. Now that prairie vole is like pudding in my hands."

"Now!" Eli pointed out. "But before that, he tore the house apart!"

Both of them gazed around the ransacked living room. The kitchen, they knew, was even worse. And who knew what sort of mess Jack had made, holed up in Victoria's office? Speaking of . . .

"Where *is* Jack?" Kevin wondered.

No sooner had he said the words than Jack burst into the room! His T-shirt was dirty and his hair was matted. His nose was dirt-smudged and his, er, aroma? It was stronger than ever.

And Jack didn't seem to care a bit. In fact, he was elated!

"I'm rich!" he cried, jumping up and down. "I'm super-rich! *Filthy* rich."

"*Tscha* on the filthy part," Eli said, curling his lip.

"Who cares!" Jack yelled. "All that matters is I am *rich*!"

"Ahem, excuse me?" Kevin cut in mildly. "But son? *How* exactly did you come into this sudden fortune? Hmmm?"

Suddenly, Jack stopped bouncing.

And smiling.

And the smug bragging? That was definitely dead in the water, too.

"Er . . ." Jack said shiftily, pulling at the neck of his T-shirt. "Well, you see . . . the thing is, Dad . . ."

"Uh-huh," Kevin said grimly. "In addition to smelling your stinkiness, Jack, I also smell a rat."

"Maybe that's the prairie voles you smell?" Jack offered helpfully.

"More like my son," Kevin said, "who's been up to no good and who's going to tell me all about it. Sit down, Jack. Make yourself comfortable. We're going to have a loooong talk."

Chapter 18

Wild Wisdom . . . *The first cloned animal was a tadpole.*

Back in the (steadily darkening) woods, Darcy was trying to calm Ginny, Sophie, and Alissa.

Not to mention herself.

"Okay," she said, "I know this looks bad, but trust me, everything's going to turn out all right."

"Then why are you wringing your hands like that?" Sophie said, pointing at Darcy's entangled fingers.

"Yeah," Ginny said, "and why is your upper lip all sweaty?"

"And look at her eyes," Alissa noted, pointing at Darcy's face. "They're darting all over the place."

"What?" Darcy said defensively. "Do the Jaybirds offer a badge for psychological profiling or something?"

When the girls just squinted at her suspiciously, Darcy threw her hands up.

"All right, all right, you've got me," Darcy said. "I

am nervous. And I feel megaguilty. I was in charge here, so it's totally my fault that we're lost."

"No," Sophie said, putting a hand on Darcy's shoulder. "Remember what I said about you treating us like equals?"

"Yeah," Darcy sighed.

"Well, that means that we all got lost together," Sophie said. "And if we work together, maybe we can find our way back, too."

"Spoken like a true leader, girlfriend," Darcy said, shooting Sophie a wobbly smile. Then she looked at all three of the girls.

"So let's use our strengths," Darcy continued. She pointed at Ginny.

"Ginny, you earned a Geographic Orientation badge on the van ride up," she said. "Do you see anything here that might put us back on track?"

Ginny frowned with concentration and looked around. She looked at the trees and looked at the ground; she looked at the sky and squinted at the sun. Then she pointed through the woods.

"That way is west," she declared with a confident nod.

"Wow!" Darcy cried. "You're like a human compass! How did you know that?"

"The sun is setting," Ginny shrugged. "The sun

sets over California, remember, Darce?"

"Oh! Oh, right," Darcy said with a relieved laugh. "Whew! Ginny, you're a lifesaver. So which way did we come from?"

"Beats me!" Ginny said with a shrug. "When we left the trail, I was too busy looking at the ground to see where the sun was."

"Ohhhh," Darcy groaned. "So we know which way is west, but we still don't know where the trail is!"

"Well, maybe . . ." Alissa offered.

"Yeah?" Darcy said eagerly.

Alissa blanched and waved her away.

"Oh, never mind," she sighed. "It's a silly idea."

"No such thing," Darcy declared. "What're ya thinking, girlfriend?"

"I'm thinking about the law of second looks," Alissa said.

Darcy cringed. "Y'know, Alissa," she said, "Sophie was right about that whole physics thing. I totally made it up. I was just trying to distract you guys from our dire straits."

"Well, just because Einstein didn't come up with it doesn't mean it's not a good idea," Alissa shrugged. "Let's take a second look at all the stuff we saw. Maybe there'll be some clues in our list."

Darcy blinked at Alissa.

"Y'know, for a pretty quiet girl," Darcy said admiringly, "you say some pretty brilliant things! That's a fab idea!"

Darcy dug the Scouts' nature list out of her pocket and smoothed it out. The Jaybirds crowded around her and they all peered at the list together.

Chestnut oak
Six-lined racerunner lizard
Tadpoles
Morel mushrooms
Ox-eyed daisies
Eastern bluebird
Buffalo clover
Celandine poppies
Rock cap moss . . .

"Okayyyy, this method isn't really working for me," Sophie said with a shrug. She looked around. "I mean, all the wildlife we've seen dashed away a minute later, leaving no markers. And the plants and stuff? I've seen a dozen clusters of buffalo clover and two dozen patches of rock cap moss. Are they the same ones we first saw? I don't have a clue."

"All the flora *does* kind of blend together, doesn't it," Darcy said, glancing around with a sigh. She slapped at a mosquito buzzing around her arm as she thought hard. She frowned at the list again.

"Hey, wait a minute," she suddenly gasped. "Tadpoles. Those are the only animals we saw that couldn't run away."

"Duh," Sophie scoffed. "They don't have legs yet."

"*Or* lungs," Darcy said. "They're a captive audience."

"Um, you've lost me there," Ginny said.

"Of course we can't go on a wild tadpole chase," Darcy explained. "But we can search for the tadpoles' *habitat*. Water! Remember? We saw the little guys in a stream that ran right alongside the trail."

"So if we find the stream, we've found our way!" Alissa cried, jumping up and down so hard, her blue beanie fell off. "So how do we find the water, Darcy?"

Darcy's elation suddenly dimmed.

"I don't know!" she admitted. "We have no shortage of good ideas, you guys. It's the follow-through that keeps getting us."

"What a total bummer," Ginny said, scratching nervously at a mosquito bite on her elbow.

"What a disaster is more like it!" Sophie said, waving away another biting bug. "And with the sun setting, it looks like the mosquitoes are getting hungry. They're gonna feast on us."

"This is so baaaaad!" Alissa cried.

Darcy was about to agree with her, when suddenly she gasped.

"Actually," she blurted with a growing grin, "it's good!"

"What?!" all three of her Jaybird charges yelled.

"You guys, what do we know about mosquitoes?" Darcy cried.

"Oh, I don't know," Sophie said sarcastically. "Why don't we start with—they're totally annoying pests?!"

"Okay, usually," Darcy admitted. "I'll give you that. But go deeper. Where do mosquitoes love to be?"

The girls pondered Darcy's riddle for a long moment. Darcy was itching (literally!) to tell them her idea, but she knew good leadership meant she had to let the Jaybirds think for themselves. So she bit her tongue while they frowned in thought.

"Hey, wait a minute!" Alissa realized suddenly. "Every time it rains, my mom asks me to go empty the extra water out of all the flower pots on our patio."

"And in the dead of summer, I can't go anywhere near the pond on our farm," Ginny pointed out, "or I'll get eaten alive."

"Because . . ." Sophie said, the answer dawning on her face along with a big grin, "mosquitoes live near water!"

"They love it!" Darcy confirmed. "And they're gonna lead us to our creek."

"Which will take us to our trail!" Alissa cried. She threw her arms around Darcy and gave her a quick hug. "I've never in my life been so excited to get bitten up by mosquitoes!"

"Oh, no," Darcy protested. "I want you guys to keep yourselves covered. If anyone's going to get bitten, it's gonna be me."

She bent over and began rolling up her khaki hiking pants, exposing plenty of skin to attract the blood-hungry insects. As she started rolling up her short shirt sleeves, she saw the three Jaybirds exchange a look.

"Maybe . . ." Ginny began a thought but let it trail off nervously.

Uh, oh, Darcy winced as she heard the doubt in Ginny's voice. *I bet I know what she's thinking: 'Maybe Darcy's not capable of getting us out of this mess—the mess she got us into!' And guess what? I'm thinking the same thing! I have no idea if this crazy follow-the-mosquitoes idea will work. Ginny's right to have no confidence in me—*

"Maybe," Ginny began again, "this would work better if we *all* rolled up our pants legs."

Darcy uttered a small gasp, then smiled at Ginny gratefully.

"You're right," she said. "Eight legs have got to be better than two! Thanks for taking a few bites for the team, you guys!"

The three Jaybirds all laughed as they rolled up their sleeves and pants.

They began walking slowly, cringing as they waited for the mosquitoes to come calling.

Slap!

Sophie grinned as she scratched a new bite.

"He came from over there!" she cried, pointing through the trees. "I saw him."

"Actually, Sophie," Darcy corrected, "it's only female mosquitoes that bite. The males are big softies. So *she* came from over there." Then Darcy added with a grin, "And *that* is great news!"

Slap! Slap!

"Ooh!" Alissa yelled happily. "I think that was one mosquito and one gnat. And they came from the same direction as Sophie's bug!"

"Let's go!" Darcy said.

The quartet began to hike toward Sophie's source.

Slap!

Darcy didn't even blink as she felt a bug bite her own leg. And when she squinted into the air, she was thrilled to see plenty of other critters flitting and swarming around.

"I really think we're on the right track," she called to the Jaybirds.

"Yay!" Sophie, Alissa, and Ginny yelled.

They also picked up the pace because the light coming through the thick treetops was growing dimmer by the minute. It became so dusky in the woods, in fact, that Darcy began having trouble seeing the ground.

She was completely guided by the buzz of the mosquitoes. When she heard them in front of her, she went straight.

When they *bzzzzzzzed* on her left, she angled her path to follow.

And when one bit her on her right leg, she angled a bit in *that* direction.

But still, the creek wasn't appearing!

Darcy looked at the Jaybirds. They were stumbling around behind her, slapping at mosquitoes as they hiked.

But are they doing the right thing, following my lead?! Darcy wondered, slumping a bit. *What if, after all the bug bites, my scheme still doesn't work? What will we do then?!*

The thought was so daunting that Darcy faltered. For a moment, she just couldn't go on. She suddenly stopped and hung her head, staring at her muddy sneakers.

"What's wrong, Darcy?" Ginny asked.

"Are we there?" Alissa cried, running up behind her. "Have we found the creek?"

"Not yet," Darcy said sadly. She slapped at another mosquito, but it seemed meaningless.

Who am I kidding? she thought. *That bug could have come from anywhere. Once again, I've failed my Jaybirds!*

When another mosquito landed on her elbow and began feasting, Darcy winced.

I deserve that, she thought. *I can't believe I got us lost in the woods!*

"Bzzzzz! Bzzzzz!"

Two gnats landed on Darcy's neck, and this time, the bites really hurt!

Okay, Darcy thought as she slapped the bugs away, *I'm not sure if I deserved that. Gimme a break, bugs!*

But the bugs didn't. More mosquitoes began dive-bombing Darcy, and a cloud of gnats began to flurry around her face.

"Ahhhh!" Darcy cried, waving her hands to try to beat the gnats away.

"That's not gonna help!" Sophie yelled to Darcy. "At least not if you just stand there! A moving target is much harder to bite. Run!"

"You're right!" Darcy yelled. "Come on!"

With the Jaybirds trotting behind her, Darcy dashed out of the buggy onslaught. She ran so fast through the darkening woods that she could barely see where she was going. Which must have been why she was completely surprised when her foot went *splat*!

"Ah!" Darcy cried, looking down. She was standing ankle-deep in a thin stream of water. A couple of tad-poles were nosing around her sneaker.

Darcy gasped and looked beyond the stream. She saw a pathway of tromped dirt and at its edge, a tree painted with a bright red slash.

"The trail!" Darcy cried, jumping up and down. Since she was still standing in the stream, she splashed her three Jaybirds with flecks of mud—not that they cared.

"You did it! You did it!" the girls cried, hopping over the stream and jumping around the trail gleefully.

"*We* did it," Darcy corrected them, happily waving off a fresh swarm of bugs. "And Ginny, you're going to make the last call of this rescue mission. How do we get back to the trailhead? This way . . ."

Darcy pointed down the trail.

". . . or that?"

Ginny looked at the setting sun, looked at the dirt beneath her feet, looked at the trees around her, and then pointed out a direction.

"Fabulous," Darcy said. She motioned to the other girls and they began walking briskly toward the trailhead. "So, Ginny, tell me," Darcy said happily, "how did you know which direction to go in?"

"Oh . . ." Ginny said slyly.

"Oh, it's a trade secret, huh?" Darcy said.

"More like, not a secret at all!" Sophie said, pointing to a sign nailed to a tree a few feet away.

TRAILHEAD, the sign said, THATAWAY. Next to the words, a big red arrow pointed in the same direction that Ginny had.

The four girls burst out laughing as they headed back to their troop.

"I never thought I'd say this," Darcy told the Jaybirds, "but I can't *wait* for the van ride home!"

Chapter 19

Wild Wisdom . . . *When a llama gets angry at another llama, it sticks its tongue out or spits at him. They'll usually spit at each other to settle an argument (usually about food), and a female llama will spit at a male llama to tell him to buzz off.*

It had been a harrowing day. When Darcy, Ginny, Alissa, and Sophie had found the rest of the Jaybird troop at the trailhead, they'd almost been buried in hugs. Victoria and the rest had been worried sick about them. April had been one step away from setting a bonfire to send the lost girls a smoke signal. And Victoria had been saddling up Oprah for a llama-led search party.

As it was, all they had to do was listen in awe as Darcy told the tale of their treacherous journey. (Okay, she might have embellished it a bit.)

When she was finished, Victoria led the troop back to the campsite, where they all broke down their tent and packed up their stuff. Before they saddled up Oprah and got ready to hike back to the van, Victoria held up her hand.

"I want to say how proud I am of Darcy, Sophie, Alissa, and Ginny for using their knowledge of nature and keeping cool heads under pressure to find their way back to us," Victoria said. "For their bravery, they'll each be awarded the Jaybird Badge of Freedom."

"Yay!" the whole troop shouted, clapping the lost party on their backs.

"But what about the Toadst Medal?" Sophie piped up.

"Oh yes, our contest," Victoria cried. "I almost forgot! Pack leaders, present your lists, please!"

Victoria scanned the three pieces of paper, counting up the teams' flora and fauna sightings.

"And the winner is . . ." Victoria said dramatically, "Lindsay and Kathi's group—Hannah and Keri!"

"Whoo hoo!" Keri cried. "We are the Jaybirds with the mostest!"

Darcy congratulated the winners before turning a sympathetic eye on Sophie.

"Sorry, girlfriend," she whispered. "I know how badly you wanted that medal."

"I thought I did," Sophie said with a shrug. "Now it seems not so important, y'know? I guess actually surviving in the wild is even more *satisfying* than getting a medal for it!"

"And you always have the story to tell," Darcy said. "That's a trophy in itself."

"Wait till we tell Kevin, Eli, and Jack," Victoria chimed in as she fed Oprah a little pre-hike grain. "They'll be so jealous! While they were ho-humming it at our house, we were having a real-life drama out here in the wilderness!"

Yeah, right.

When Victoria, Darcy, and Lindsay staggered into the house after dropping off Kathi and the Jaybird Scouts, they found a flurry of activity!

Jack—his hair wet from a recent bath—was glumly sanding and staining the kitchen chairs. Eli was spackling a bunch of holes in the living-room wall. Kevin was in the kitchen, putting new bins of flour and sugar into the pantry and mopping the sticky, messy floor.

"What is going on here?" Victoria cried with a sleepy smile. "Kevin, I only asked you to take care of our farm animals! This is way beyond the call of duty."

"Ohhhh, I wouldn't speak too soon, Victoria," Kevin said, plunking his mop back into the soapy bucket. "You see, our overnight at your house wasn't nearly as idyllic as your camping trip."

"That's funny," Darcy said. "We were thinking that our campout wasn't nearly as idyllic as your overnight here!"

"Har, har, har," Jack said grumpily as he sanded away.

Victoria arched an eyebrow and said, "Something tells me there's more to this story than meets the eye."

"Yeah, there's more," Eli said from his perch on the stepladder. "Eight *more* members of your household, to be exact."

"Excuse me?" Darcy said. "Don't tell me you let the paparazzi hang out here! We've always told them they can camp out on the front yard, but the house is off-limits! Those guys never wipe their feet!"

"Actually," Kevin said, "your new houseguests are quite a bit smaller."

He led Darcy and Victoria over to the hall closet and showed them the prairie vole family, which was contentedly snoozing away.

"Aw, but those were my favorite Skechers!" Darcy complained, pointing at Mrs. Vole's shoe nest.

"And they will be again," Kevin said with a smile, "in about six weeks, when the vole babies are big enough to leave their nest."

Darcy sighed.

"How did this happen?" she demanded.

"Oh, I imagine it was just an innocent mishap," Victoria said with a wink. "You know, sort of like straying from your hiking trail when you were specifically told not to?"

While Lindsay stifled a laugh, Darcy hung her head.

"Point taken," she said. "The voles can have custody of my Skechers until they're grown. They *are* kind of cute."

"Unlike my brother," Lindsay said as the group walked back into the kitchen. Jack was still sanding, muttering angrily to himself as he worked. "What's he sulking about?"

"Let's just say," Kevin said, "that you don't need paparazzi when you've got Jack around."

"Huh?" Darcy and Victoria said together.

"Go on, Jack," Kevin said sternly. "Tell them why you've been so smelly for the past twenty-four hours."

"Only getting more confused," Darcy said, shaking her head.

Jack stopped sanding and hung his head.

"I pulled stuff out of your garbage can," he admitted, "and sold it on eBay."

"What?!" Victoria cried.

"Gross," Darcy said.

"If you ask me," Jack said sullenly, "I should be

commended for my entrepreneurial spirit. I made a fortune!"

"Just how large is this fortune?" Victoria said, crossing her arms over her chest.

"Oh, you'll find out," Kevin cut in, "when Jack donates his proceeds to the Jaybird Scout Troop 117! Your next camping trip will be paid for by Mr. Jack Adams."

"As soon as I get paid for your gourmet butter wrapper, your used-up calendar, and Darcy's stack of old *Pop People* magazines," Jack said.

"Jack," Lindsay said, rolling her eyes, "you are so—"

"Weird!" Eli finished for her.

"Well, I'd say the punishment fits the crime," Victoria said, giving Jack's damp head a pat. She turned to Darcy and Lindsay. "And I suppose our next overnight will be a bit more luxurious than the last!"

"What, we'll have *two* llamas along?" Lindsay joked—until she glanced at Darcy, whose face was stony. "Or maybe," Lindsay added quietly, "we'll have one more llama and one less Darcy."

To tell the truth, Darcy had been thinking the exact same thing—until she heard Lindsay voice her thoughts out loud. Then, before she had a chance to think about it, Darcy blurted, "No way!"

"Really?!" Lindsay said happily.

Really? Darcy asked herself.

 **DARCY'S DISH**

Really! Don't ask me how this change of heart happened. I mean, if anything made my wilderness allergy flare back up, it was getting myself and three nine-year-old girls lost in the woods. And as for the llama spit, the worms, the fish fiasco, and the franks and beans? Let's not even go there . . . because if you overlook those things and just consider the company on our camping trip? Then you've gotta admit—it rocked! I guess it's true what they say: It doesn't matter where you go but who goes with you.

As long as they keep their Jaybird calls to themselves!